The Plan

A Story of Redemption

Jeannie G. Bruenning

PROLOGUE

Chaos had overtaken the entire Kingdom. The sounds of people yelling and shouting blended together with the pleading and wailing of the loved ones they were leaving behind. It was so loud that Konnory couldn't make out his own footsteps on the stone floor, as he sprinted up the stairs and down the hall towards the Dining Room. The mayhem had given birth to a darkness that was quickly enveloping the Kingdom.

The King and Queen looked up as Konnory rushed through the door into the Dining Room. Without a word, he walked over to the Queen, leaned over and gave her a kiss on the cheek. "Mother," he said softly. She did not reply other than simply nodding her head in acknowledgement. Konnory walked behind the King and took the empty chair next to him. "Magnor has reported," Konnory said.

"Is he still with the troops?" the King asked.

"Yes, he is. He has ordered that no one is to prevent anyone from leaving. A few have already challenged that command. Now, they stand together and watch as family and friends walk through the gates." Konnory's head dropped.

"I know it is agonizing. This will be the most difficult experience of their lives. The choice to leave is theirs. Holding anyone back will not be tolerated," the King said, as he reached out and took the Queen's hand.

With each moment, the crowd heading towards the gates grew. The gate was opened and a flood of figures began pouring out into the Darkness. Above the roar, there were shouts of triumph and screams of anguish.

The Dining Room door opened once again. Carasi stood holding a ledger. "Father, Magnor has reported that there are those within the ranks of the captains that have left. It also seems that Waldemar has left." The King closed his eyes, and the Queen gripped his hand tighter. "Do you want to put an end to this?" Carasi asked.

"We must not," the King replied. "They are each making the choice for themselves. We will honor their free will to do so."

"But Father, we are losing so many!" Carasi protested. "They don't understand that once they are outside of those gates…"

"No," interrupted the Queen. She spoke gently but with great authority. "There is no other option but to honor their choice." Carasi bowed his head and took his leave. As he opened the door, a wave of shouts from outside flooded the room.

The castle itself had almost entirely emptied of people. Trays of food and bottles of wine had been left on shelves by attendants who had rushed outside to see what was happening. Servants had abandoned their brooms and mops as they sprinted home to check on loved ones. Scattered piles of papers and documents lay strewn across the Throne Room bearing witness to where the King's advisors and scribes had been standing when the shouting began.

"He has done great damage," the King said. His words brought a weight of certainty and heaviness into the room. "Konnory, go find your brothers, no one should be alone on this day."

Konnory hesitated, not wanting to leave them or to leave the security that the Dining Room embodied. Eventually, he found the strength to stand and walked out into the storm.

"He has done as he threatened," said the Queen.

"Yes, my dear. Patho has waged his war and taken his prisoners. When the last one has left and the gates close, that is when the real battle begins," said the King.

"Are you sure it is a battle we want to fight?" the Queen asked ever so gently.

"This is not about what I want to do," the King said, as he raised the Queen's hand to his lips and kissed it. Another wave of shouting was heard just outside the window. The cries of mourning and screams of anguish continued well into the night.

To the Fallen Souls who have not realized the need for forgiveness,
May your journey lead you back to the King.

Chapter One

"Redeem who? Don't tell me we're discussing this again?" Magnor said as he entered the Dining Room, interrupting the discussion of those sitting around the table. It was impossible for Magnor to enter any room unnoticed. He was tall, standing almost a head above the rest of the world. The only person Magnor ever had to look up to was his youngest brother, Jael. From the time Magnor could walk, he had been groomed to be King. His posture, stride, and stature were that of nobility. No one ever needed to question his lineage; he exuded royalty with every movement.

Magnor walked to the end of the table, making eye contact with each of his four brothers. No one at the table was eager to have him join the conversation. They had been over this many times and were all very clear on his stance. "I thought I made myself understood the last time you brought this up," he focused in on Jael waiting for a response. Jael glanced up, smiled and winked. Magnor stiffened. "I hate when you do that!" he said.

"I know," Jael replied. "That's what makes it so enjoyable."

"This is your doing isn't it?" Magnor barked in his commander voice. "Why can't you leave it alone?"

"Magnor," the King interrupted, "welcome home! Come in my son, have a seat," the King motioned to an empty chair next to him and away from Jael. "How were your travels? I trust you found everything in order?"

"Yes, Father, all is in order." Magnor broke his stare on Jael but not before he gave one last glare. "The captains are doing an excellent job." He made his way to the end of the long dining table. Even Magnor's walk drew attention; each step was full of determination and purpose. "I'm not sure if I have ever seen the troops looking so prepared. I trust Mother has returned?" he asked, taking the chair next to the King.

"Yes, she has," Father said. "She also commented on the strength and unity of the troops."

"The troops are always honored by her presence. It was good having her there." Magnor reached for the carafe to fill his goblet. Pivoting in his chair to face the other four seated at the table, he said, "Now, why has the redemption plan resurfaced? I thought we were finished with it."

Each of his four brothers had returned to their work and seemed deeply engrossed in that which lay in front of them. They were either truly engrossed or simply pretending in hopes that Magnor would move on. Carasi briefly glanced up. Sounding most uninterested, he responded, "Yes, it has resurfaced. Jael continues to receive requests from the Fallen Souls pleading for forgiveness. He believes we need to investigate every possibility." He turned the ledger page and continued working.

Most of Carasi's days were spent looking over ledgers such as this one. He held the responsibility of overseeing the daily operations of the Kingdom. Hundreds of people reported to him throughout the day. Rarely was he found without a ledger or stacks of ledgers within reach.

The King and Queen had reigned over this Kingdom from the beginning of time. Their sons knew only of this life. Magnor was the warrior, Carasi and Ferrul the business minds, Konnory and Jael, the youngest, were creative, thinkers, and if left to their own devises, followed their hearts more than their heads.

Magnor knew that this had not been an impromptu conversation, as Carasi didn't have time for such things. "Don't you have more important things to fill your time?" Magnor advised Carasi, who never looked up. "They're gone, let them be gone."

Ferrul sat across from Carasi. These two seemed inseparable at times. Their brothers argued that they shared the same brain and from time to time took bets as to who was in use of it. They frequently finished each others sentences. However, neither felt speaking was a necessary way to communicate. It was only required when dealing with those of inefficient intelligence. Ferrul and Carasi appeared to know what the other was thinking.

Ferrul shared many of Carasi's responsibilities. However, Carasi focused on the financial structure of the Kingdom and Ferrul on the operational. Ferrul was blankly staring at the figures on the page. One would have thought that he was unaware that Magnor had even entered the room. His thoughts were a great distance away.

"I just don't understand," Ferrul said in a tone barely above his breath. With eyes blankly fixed on the page, he sat motionless except for a slight shaking of his head. He rolled the marble pen between his fingers and then softly tapped the page with it. "They had it all," he paused again, taking time to remember. Sitting back in his chair, he rubbed his chin and gazed up at the ceiling. "No, it's true they did not have the family name, but aside from that, they had it all. Nothing was withheld from them. Nothing would have been denied them. If they wanted for anything, if they needed anything, all they had to do was ask."

The room was silent except for the gentle percussion of Ferrul's pen. Magnor looked around the table. The expressions and determination he saw in his brothers irritated him. He slid his chair back breaking the silence. He took a sip from his goblet. Anger and frustration consumed his expression. He thought they had put this discussion to rest weeks ago. He so wanted it to end. There was too much lost, too many crushed dreams, too many unanswered questions, too much pain. Why did Jael keep it alive? Why couldn't he let it go? Why were they talking about this yet again? He wanted to scream, "They're gone and there isn't anything we can do about it. It was their choice. Let them suffer!" He wanted to scream, but he didn't. There was just too much pain and besides, he had been here before, and he knew his brothers well; none of them would let this go until all were convinced it was the right decision.

"He is very good at what he does." Konnory said gazing toward Jael, yet a million miles away. "We all know that." Konnory stood and made his way to the window. "It's just a shame that what Patho does - is deceit." He leaned against the window sill looking out. He scanned the gardens below as if he was looking for someone.

None of them could help remember the events leading up to that day long past. Patho had been in such an uproar. He and his recruits had made their way through the Kingdom shouting lies and promises, threats and opportunities. They created chaos wherever they went. Every minute his supporters grew in number. Patho was good at deceit. He was the best. He drew them in, spread his lies, and offered a way of escape without anyone knowing they were being lead astray. He had a way to make even the most secure person question their own minds. Then, at the end of it all, when Patho finally demanded the King let them go, there seemed no other choice.

No one expected that Patho would take so many with him. It took months to register how many Patho had deceived; how many souls he had stolen; how many he caused to fall. The mass exodus shook the Kingdom to it's core. No one was untouched by that day and it's effects were still being felt.

☙

Patho had once held a high rank in the Kingdom. He was known as the Angel of Light. He was the keeper of all wisdom and knowledge. There were those who shared their concerns with the King that Patho may someday see himself as equal. The King quickly dismissed such a notion, reminding them that Patho did not own vast wisdom or knowledge, he was only the keeper of it. It belonged fully to the King. "Also," the King would say with a sort of all knowing smile, "Patho cannot see the future, his only vantage point is the past and the immediate." This left those voicing their concerns with an uneasy satisfaction.

Patho was content in his position as the Angel of Light, keeper of all wisdom and knowledge. He mastered excellent communication skills. He also possessed the talent to encourage, instill insight, speak boldly, and motivate. He delighted in bringing forces together, imparting his knowledge to them, and motivating them to do good. That was his duty. That was his calling. That was his satisfaction. Until one day it wasn't. He realized he was such a great motivator that he no longer had to participate. He could simply encourage, instruct and give direction. Everyone did as he said without him lifting a finger, batting an eyelash, never-mind breaking a sweat.

It didn't happen overnight, it was a gradual decline. Patho became bolder and bolder when giving instructions, at the same time, feeling the need to do less and less. Eventually, his tone changed. He no longer was an encourager, he bordered on dictator. He practiced raising his voice ever so slightly. Over the course of time, he learned he could shout the loudest and most threatening commands and no one thought it bad. Well almost no one. Those who did, found themselves reassigned ever so quickly.

Such behavior made him feel as if he had authority. His realization that he could motivate anyone into doing almost anything he wanted surprised and delighted him. How far could he take this, he often wondered. There was no reason he was not equal to the King. He began to believe that he possessed all the wisdom and knowledge in the universe. He could get anyone to do anything he wished.

And he could. Patho tested his abilities in small ways. He wondered if he could ever motivate his followers to go against their own hopes and beliefs. Certainly he had the talent required. Little by little, he learned to move, motivate and guide his followers ever so gently into actions they once felt were wrong.

Patho knew if used correctly, he could motivate the unwilling to be willing. He could move the unmovable. He could change the minds and hearts of the King's servants just enough for them to question the King's authority and love. Motivation is a commendable skill, until it becomes manipulation. Patho was undoubtedly the greatest manipulator in the Kingdom.

The day came when he realized the enormous power he possessed due to his motivational strength. He also realized his possibilities were endless. It wasn't long before he had his eyes set on the throne. Patho wasted no time in creating his plan. He spent time laying the groundwork, instilling doubt and question in the minds of the King's subjects. He formed his inner circle from the group of individuals he had honed his most recent skills on. He made promises of a new kingdom, his kingdom. And to his inner circle, he promised positions as Warlords and other high ranks.

Patho held the first meeting with his anxious and newly appointed Warlords in a room located below the stables. It was little more than a walkway set between the two chambers that housed the horse manure. They crouched on the dirt floor. Above them were large beams, the only thing separating them from the horses. In a strange way, Patho thought it felt quite comfortable.

Patho began the meeting: "I had you come here today to begin our plans for the final attack. I have hand-selected you to lead the battle to freedom." They had been handpicked, but not because of their strengths. Rather, Patho's ability to get them to do anything he asked. "I have spent a great deal of time laying the foundation for this attack. I have had countless and seemingly endless – and let's not forget - meaningless conversations with half of the King's idiots – or should I say - leaders." The Warlords snickered in a very childish manner.

"The King will not relinquish his throne to me. And we are too few in number to overtake him. Instead, I plan to ask, or should I say DEMAND?" Those in attendance cheered once again. "I am DEMANDING that the King allow us to leave the Kingdom."

The small group hailed their new leader, and the horses stomped their hoofs from above. No one questioned where they were going, but they were ready to go!

"We aren't going alone!" Patho said over another round of cheers. We are going to persuade multitudes to join us and leave the King's control!" The small group were beside themselves with adoration."I am convinced that upon our exit, we will successfully rid the Kingdom of its inhabitants." A loud cheer rang through the rafters, startling the horses once again and creating the sound of thunder above. The cheers from his Warlords combined with the noise from above gave Patho a burst of confidence. "I have created our battle cry!" Pulling a single piece of paper from inside his coat pocket, he read aloud each line with great emphasis.

1.We promise freedom from bondage.
2.We promise great opportunity for battle and warfare.
3.We promise great wealth: castles and servants for all.
4.We promise no consequences for your actions.

Another cheer rang out from the group. This time, Patho quieted them quickly in fear of drawing attention to their gathering. "Who shall deliver these promises?" asked one of the more excitable Warlords.

"We need a great motivator, someone who is terribly convincing. We need the best motivator in the Kingdom," responded Patho.

"You are the greatest motivator in the-"

"I accept," Patho said before the Warlord could finish the compliment. "We must work quickly; I need all of you to start spreading our promises as soon as you leave here." 'Never do what you can get others to do for you,' was one of Patho's many mottos. "I'll begin in the morning. No, perhaps mid-day. Yes. That will be much better." Patho felt it a waste of time to begin the day early. It was far better to start later and end later. He had also found that his victims were much more receptive to his motivations after they had expended their energy on daily tasks. He greatly disagreed with the notion that people were at their best in the early hours of the day, he found them much more agreeable later on. "I'll personally attend to the castle in order to add to our numbers."

The next day, he did just that. Patho made his way through the castle, shouting his promises while his Warlords made their way through the Kingdom echoing his words. Patho was well prepared for his attack on the castle. He knew that within its walls were the King's closest and most respected subjects. Patho had spent time setting the stage. He had initiated several individual conversations; each offered a very persuasive argument customized to motivate. All of which questioned the King's authority, decisions and possible sanity.

The King was not the only one he attacked-- the Princes had been included in these accusations. Patho knew he had successfully instilled question and doubt in the minds of many. In this final attack, he desired to create an overwhelming amount of chaos and instill just enough fear to cause them to question the King enough to leave.

On that fateful day, Patho was the first to walk through the gates surrounding the Kingdom. Following him was a flood of deceived. No one knew for sure what lay beyond the Kingdom walls. They knew that any area past the gates of the Kingdom was unprotected. What they were unaware of was that there did not exist a place outside of the King's authority. Inside the gates there was protection, provision, and most importantly, the King himself. Beyond were Darkness and the unknown.

Gazing out the window, Konnory relived that day. He thought it was impossible to ever forget the scene as he watched a flood of individuals blindly following Patho through the gates. Returning his attention back to the group, he continued, "He tried to deceive all of us. No one was off limits. We lost so many."

Chapter Two

We lost too many," Jael said in his gentle manner. "The final count still has not been completed. We do know that there isn't a region, area, or family that was not affected," Carasi said without looking up from the ledger.

"Yes, and we know the effects," said Ferrul as his eyes fell on the empty chairs in the room. Jael followed his glances. "It was devastating to all of us, especially to know that members of our own family could be so deceived." There was a dark heaviness that blanketed the room. This had once been the room they had met together to share meals, tell of the days adventures, talk of the future. Each chair that circled the large table belonged to a member of the family. Each should have been filled. The empty chairs magnified the absences of those they loved. Those they had grown up with. Those they called brother. No one was ever able to talk about that dreadful day without feeling the pain of loss.

Jael took a deep breath. He tightened his jaw and gently pounded the table with his fist, as though it were a gavel, "We need a plan. We continue to receive written requests pleading for forgiveness from those that followed Patho. They are willing to do anything to redeem themselves." Magnor stiffened as the words filled the room.

The requests began arriving immediately after Patho had made his great departure. He had promised so much to those who were willing to follow him, but it had all been lies. As soon as they had left the Kingdom, they realized he had nothing to offer. In fact, from what Jael could piece together from the requests, Patho had left them on their own from the very beginning.

When word had come to the King that such requests were arriving, Jael immediately took on the task of reading them. Each painted a picture of hopelessness and despair. Each was offered by someone who had willingly walked out of the Kingdom. They were filled with remorse and pleas for forgiveness. Each request broke his heart. While discussing the requests for forgiveness and reinstatement back into the Kingdom, Jael referred to those who had left as the "Fallen Souls." The name stuck.

"Do you believe we have heard from all of them?" Konnory inquired as he returned to his seat.

"No, unfortunately, not all of them," Jael lowered his head for a moment. As he looked back up, he turned his attention to Konnory. "There are still many who continue to be deceived by his lies and promises. However, there are those who greatly regret their decision. They are pleading for forgiveness. They are agonizing over the choice they made and appear willing to do whatever it takes to get out of Patho's control. We must do something."

"Do something?!" Magnor said. He pushed back his chair and sprang to his feet. "This was an isolated event! There is no protocol for this situation. It's just not going to happen. No one who has ever left the Kingdom has asked to return. We have never before needed such a plan. It does not exist."

Konnory reached out and grabbed Magnor's sleeve, pulling him back to his seat. Magnor resisted momentarily, but eventually settled back into his chair. Konnory turned to Jael and said, "Jael, can you tell by the requests, what exactly they are looking for? Is it only forgiveness? Do they want redemption? Do they think they will be welcomed back as if nothing ever happened?" Being the philosopher in the group, Konnory desired to see all sides of any situation. He had great insight and his counsel was wise. It was important for him to understand the full intent of the requests.

"I do not believe they are looking for full and complete restoration." Jael was gentle in his response.

"Good!" Magnor blurted out.

Undeterred by Magnor's response, Jael continued. "From the requests I have seen, the Fallen Souls are willing to do anything, anything. If redemption requires them to be the lowest in the Kingdom, they are willing. In fact, the last requests I saw, they were pleading for forgiveness; even if they are not allowed back into the Kingdom." Jael paused. It was evident that he was greatly concerned. "The longer they are out there, the more they are filled with hopelessness. I don't believe any of them think there is any chance of being restored to their previous positions. I would say they are so remorseful of their own actions that they have become unsure of their own abilities. Forgiveness is what drives them; it's what they are longing for."

The King turned toward Jael, "Are they making these requests on their own?"

The room was silent. Jael glanced across the table at the empty chair that sat directly in front of him, "For the most part, they are individual requests. But there is one who seems to be organizing them." Jael took a long pause, "Of the requests I have seen, the request that forces me to keep this discussion going...came from Quaine."

The stillness of the room was palpable. The King had lost a host of subjects that day. He had lost advisors. He had lost warriors. The King's heart ached for each one who had fallen. But what caused him unbearable pain was the loss of Quaine and Palti, his sons.

"Did he mention his brother?" asked the King as he was either unable or unwilling to call them by name.

"Father," Jael could see the pain and love in his eyes, "he mentions several by name. It appears that there is great support for his effort to find forgiveness."

"Has there been any word of...."

"No, Father, no one has mentioned Palti." Jael bowed his head as the words left his lips. Palti's loss was deeply felt by each. Jael looked around the table at all who were seated there. He spoke out of love, loss and determination, "They are all lost forever unless we create a plan for redemption, a plan that allows them to return home."

Magnor pushed his chair back, this time very much in control. He stood to his feet and began to pace, "Redemption requires sacrifice, great sacrifice. The sacrifice must be given freely. A sacrifice of this magnitude is almost inconceivable." He walked to the far end of the room and stood in front of the fireplace. He turned and looked back at the group, "You all must understand that if we move forward, we must move carefully. Any mistake, any decision made outside the guidelines of justice could possibly open the door for - that fool - to do more damage." To the other's amazement, this was the first hint that Magnor could be persuaded.

"Patho has made his choice and he will not change. He has one goal and one goal only: to dethrone me and take over the Kingdom."

"That will never happen!" Carasi's voice boomed as he slammed his hand on the table. Carasi was small in stature, but he spoke with authority. He was honest, direct and decisive. No one equaled his confidence. When Carasi spoke, he spoke out of knowledge. He didn't make assumptions and never answered unless confident he had the facts to back up his statements.

"We didn't think any of this would ever happen!" Ferrul corrected.

Magnor paced and the King sat with his eyes closed. No one spoke. They wanted to; each wanted to boldly express their opinions, but they had all been here before. They had all been a part of this conversation; in fact, this conversation had begun and ended many times. The five brothers realized that battling it out one more time would not get them closer to a solution. As the King slowly opened his eyes, he once again scanned the room. There were empty chairs, each representing someone who no longer lived under his protection. He looked at each of his sons, each one acknowledging him in return.

"Magnor, you are correct that a plan of redemption will require great sacrifice; greater than perhaps any of you can imagine. Sacrifice must be offered willingly. No apprehensions, no force; it must be from a pure heart, of pure intent." The King paused. The room was silent besides the sounds of Magnor's steps. "They walked away for a handful of empty promises. We will all have to make sacrifices to bring them back." The King turned to gaze out the window. He knew that none of them, perhaps even himself, could truly comprehend the degree of such sacrifice.

There was but a moment of hesitation before the Princes burst forth in conversation. It started calmly but quickly turned into an emotion-filled discussion. Magnor was voicing his great disapproval. Ferrul and Carasi were discussing whether or not a sufficient sacrifice could even be obtained, and Konnory found himself being pulled into both conversations.

Jael rose to his feet and began to walk the perimeter of the room. He was so familiar with this place. His family had gathered here for as long as he could remember. Before the Princes were allowed to participate in the discussions held in the Throne Room, the Dining Room had been their meeting place.

Every other room of the castle housed elegantly appointed pieces, crafted out of the finest material. Gold, silver, and bronze trimmed every room. The King and Queen intended the castle to represent all that was good in the Kingdom. If one looked hard enough, you could find every material available. But the Dining Room was different. The King had wanted this to be a place that represented the bond that he had with his sons. Unlike the other rooms in the castle, which were ornate and majestic, the Dining Room was to be bold and strong. The King designed the Dining Room using only three materials: wood, iron and stone.

Around the perimeter of the room were pieces of stately wood furnishings, hand-carved with the greatest detail. Each one could be used as serving pieces when the room housed a celebration, party or informal meeting. The table ran the length of the room. It, too, was made of wood. Time was spent selecting the strongest of wood. Each panel of the table was a single cut. Over the table hung candelabras forged out of iron. Around the table were nine hand-carved chairs. There was no doubt as to which ones belonged to the King and Queen. Each of the other chairs was designed specifically for each son. Jael remembered the smaller, less elaborate chairs they had used as boys. When the time came for each son to be promoted to a position of honor and responsibility, they were presented with a new chair. These new chairs had been carved to express the personality of each Prince.

Windows lined the room. They reached floor to ceiling allowing for the most perfect view of the gardens. On the far wall, the King had designed a stone fireplace. As a child, Jael remembered it being large enough to allow him and his six brothers to play in, tracking soot and ash throughout the castle. Chairs sat on either side of the hearth, Jael had fond memories of sitting in front of the fire as Father read one of his favorite books from the royal library. Jael loved this room and the memories that it held. Of any room in the castle, this one represented comfort and safety.

Today, they were no longer children; each had grown into the title they held: Prince. Each was unique in his appearance and abilities. This is what Jael appreciated the most about his brothers. Magnor had great strength, not only physically but also in character. He was a natural leader. Father said it was so from the beginning. Magnor carried himself with dignity. He respected his position and all the responsibility that came with it.

Carasi was a diligent student. His great knowledge and love for numbers made him a very black and white thinker. No matter how hard he tried, Carasi never seemed to be able to pretend or imagine. He was guided by facts and needed to prove every theory. If Carasi said it was possible, you could bet your life on it.

Carasi and Ferrul made an incredible team. Ferrul had great insight. He could see every detail of a plan before it was ever written. If Carasi said an idea could be successful, Ferrul told you exactly how it should be done. Most of the time, these two brothers worked as one. They were united in thought.

Konnory saw every situation from both sides. Life was far from black and white for Konnory. He lived in the gray. He was the philosopher. Konnory may have acquired all of Carasi's imagination. Konnory brought dimension to discussions. He offered alternative viewpoints when decisions were being made. Konnory also had a great sense of humor, a trait that took many by surprise. It seemed to be such a contradiction; philosopher and comic. No matter the severity of a situation, somewhere in Konnory's mind, he could see the humor of it.

Jael stood in front of the fireplace. He looked at Quaine and Palti's empty chairs. He felt the emptiness. The pain was still so real. He would do anything for his brothers. He would do anything for all of those who had fallen. They had to do something. They could not leave these desperate souls lost forever. He would do anything. Jael cleared his throat, "Father, I would be willing to do whatever it takes." His words echoed through the room and silenced the others.

"Jael, my son, you don't know what you are saying. Even if you fully understood this level of sacrifice, I'm not sure that I'm willing to take the risk. Jael, you must take time to think this through, we all must."

"I have Father." Jael walked to the King's side and knelt on one knee. He placed his hand on the King's forearm. He looked up into the all knowing, all loving face of his Father, "I have thought of this since the moment it happened. I don't understand their decision. I can't imagine what they were thinking when they walked away. But, if there is anything we can do that will allow Quaine and Palti and those who have fallen from your grace and from your Kingdom to find peace, I am willing." Jael's voice was filled with emotion, "They are wandering aimlessly: lost, grieving and desperate."

He looked around the table. He had the full attention of each of his brothers. As he locked eyes with Magnor, he stopped. He saw his brother's pain. Magnor did his best to hide it, but it was there. "They are not just Fallen Souls as we refer to them so often. They have names." Magnor was expressionless as he looked at his brother. "Yes, Father, I have thought about this. It's all I think about, in fact."

"Jael, are you serious? You would be willing to put everything at risk?" Konnory questioned.

"Yes, Konnory, I am willing." The King put his hand on Jael's hand.

Silence filled the room once again. The King looked at each empty chair and then down to Jael. "Let us begin to outline a plan. This is not to say that such a plan will be possible or acceptable, but without at least an outline, we are unable to make any further decisions."

Jael leaned forward, "Thank you, Father." Jael bowed his head.

Carasi pulled out an empty tablet. There was no handbook on redemption. None had ever been needed. The only book that could help them was the one created just after that dreadful day. It was a ledger containing the names of those who were fallen, a list of the Fallen Souls.

The King removed his hand from Jael's and the two locked eyes. The corner of Jael's mouth turned up slightly as he nodded his head toward his Father. A teary mist formed over the King's eyes.

Carasi picked up his pen and wrote the words 'The Plan' at the top of his tablet.

Chapter Three

C reating The Plan was the first time these six men had cooperatively engaged in a single cause. Each one had personal reasons for such a plan. They were unified in its purpose. There was a level of focus and determination they had never experienced. Seeing his sons working side by side for one single purpose made him see them, perhaps for the first time, as the strong, intelligent leaders they had become. They were no longer boys. They had become men, leaders, Princes.

They were all in agreement that assistance from outside the group would be limited. The Plan had to be kept a secret. Should the word reach the Fallen Souls that such an attempt was being made, there was no telling what the reaction would be. They were certain that if word got out within the Kingdom, it would quickly spread, and in doing so, had the potential of doing more harm than good.

The Queen participated from a distance. She felt strongly this was a mission that needed to be under the control of the King and her sons. The King kept her well informed of the details. The daily responsibilities of the Kingdom were taken over by the Queen allowing full attention to be focused on The

Plan. She was entirely as capable as the King, in fact besides differentiating their voices, no one was ever aware when one took over for the other. These Royals had become one long ago, and each lived and breathed for the other. There was never a doubt in anyones mind that the Queen was the King's equal.

Magnor was the only one who continued to voice any reluctance. He wasn't sure of his willingness to welcome back those who had left the Kingdom. He resented spending time creating a plan that would offer forgiveness to the Fallen Souls. As a warrior, he felt it would have been better to spend this time creating plans and experimenting with security measures to ensure that such a thing would never happen again. In the end, he had given his seal of approval, but he resisted with great force. It took all the determination of the other four to keep the process moving forward.

After great deliberations, they finalized an outline that passed all of their approval. Through their discussion and debate, the King gave his approval with two additions: He held the right to bring an end to The Plan, and he would be responsible for its final phase.

The Princes saw the wisdom in the first, but the last left an uneasiness in them.

As the final round of argument turned into agreement, Ferrul collected the files and papers that found themselves spread across the table. "We have strategized," Ferrul began, "and are prepared for as much as is within our control. No matter how defined it is, or how well it is executed, it is still a very vulnerable plan." It was late in the evening. Dinner had been served and was now replaced with fruit, cheese, and bread platters. A large plate of dark chocolate delicacies sat in the middle of the table. A wine steward was always close by, assuring the carafes and King's goblet would never lack.

"Father, let's seal up Patho and his followers once and for all." Magnor said, as he replenished his goblet and took a piece of chocolate, making his way to the fireplace. "You could have done that from the beginning. I would have put an end to this nonsense long ago!"

"You would have been willing to lose forever all those souls?" Konnory asked, as he reached for the carafe sitting in the middle of the table. He filled his goblet. Taking a handful of dates, he settled back in his chair and focused his attention toward Magnor. The others knew he was priming his brother for a rather heated debate.

Magnor was ready for action. He spun around to address Konnory. In the process, his glance passed over to the King whose look made it clear that no such debate would happen this evening. With a firm sense of authority Magnor replied, "We have already lost them! They made their choice. No one forced them. They walked away freely. And because of it, we've been forced to offer a way of escape." Magnor took a sip of wine. "I'm still don't believe we have to do this." Raising his glass he said, "This is a battle we should be fighting! Not sitting here - preparing."

"Magnor, that's enough. The time for argument and discussion is over. We have all invested a great deal in this plan. If anything is going to work, it will be this," Carasi said, as he took a stack of papers from Ferrul.

"I have been ready to end this so many times, Magnor," the King said.

"What!" echoed in the minds of his sons. "Been willing to end this? End what? Why hadn't he?"

The King calmed their angst as he continued. "I've agonized over this decision. Your Mother knows. We've spent endless hours discussing our options." He tore a piece of bread from a large loaf and covered it with his favorite cheese, "To be honest, I've come very close to overruling all of you and putting an end to this idea." The King sat back in his chair, looked at the miniature sandwich he had just created, and took a bite.

"Anytime Father! I'll back that decision with all our troops," Magnor offered.

Jael was seated on the far end of the table. He had been engrossed in a newly delivered stack of requests. As he read through them, he had only been partially listening to the discussion, but Father's words had caught him off guard. He knew Father had not given his approval quickly, but he was unaware that the King had considered putting an end to it. The Kings words had his complete attention.

"Father?" Jael said.

Holding his hand out to quiet his son, the King continued, "Jael's conviction in this matter and his determination to provide a way for our lost brothers, our lost friends, and fellow soldiers, has won me over." The King took another bite, finishing the sandwich. Placing his hands on the arms of his chair, he adjusted his position. "Let it be known and let there be no mistake, this is the ONE plan." Raising his finger to emphasize his words, he leaned forward. "There will be one and only one opportunity for forgiveness. After this, there will be no second chances. This is a very just plan."

"It's more than fair," Magnor mumbled from the far corner of the room.

"After this, I will bring an end to Patho's threats and control," The King said settling back again. "The plan for Patho's captivity was created prior to his departure. He will not win that battle. He may feel as if he has authority over the Darkness, but he only has it because I have allowed him to survive. This plan is an attempt to reclaim those that he has deceived. If this one act will allow us to minimize his damage by redeeming those we have loved, then let it be so. There will be no further talk of options. The Plan is complete. Let us be in agreement. From this moment on, we move forward." There was a new level of commitment and certainty in the King's voice, and it did not go unnoticed by anyone in the room.

Ferrul handed Carasi the last of the files. "It is time to begin." Ferrul stood and gestured for the rest to join him. "I have arranged for our transport to meet us here at dawn. Our provisions have been sent ahead and all should be in place when we arrive. Communication has been set up here. This will be the first time all of us have journeyed from the castle together, which in itself is a risk. But we believe any and all foreseen dangers have security in place." Ferrul looked toward Carasi for confirmation.

"Yes," responded Carasi, "all is in place, we are ready to begin." Carasi handed the boxes containing files to his attendant, and with a nod, the attendant made his way to the door. "Now let us retire. Morning is a few short hours away. Tomorrow we begin our journey to the edge of the Kingdom. Father has decided the location of this new kingdom."

"New kingdom? You can hardly call it a kingdom!" Konnory replied as he settled back into his chair. It didn't appear that anyone besides Ferrul and Carasi were eager to retire.

Ferrul was already to the door when he turned to answer. Realizing that no one else in the room had moved, he looked at Carasi and rolled his eyes. "True, it's not a kingdom as we know it," he responded, "but for those who choose, it will serve as their kingdom as long as they remain there."

"Choose to live there? That is still such a ludicrous concept," Magnor said as he reached for the carafe that the wine steward had just delivered. "I vote they get a reward just for being able to tolerate it," he said. The King let out a puff of laughter. Magnor's sarcasm was, at times, entertaining.

"Are we really still discussing this?" Carasi asked looking at his brothers in disbelief. "Yes, it's their only choice," he said quite firmly. "It's their only real option. We can't possibly allow them back into the Kingdom without redemption, and there is no way they will find redemption outside the Kingdom. We have to establish a neutral place. Any of the Fallen Souls who are requesting forgiveness will be allowed to inhabit this new world; or as we have decided to call it - Turayn." Carasi was delivering his lines as if rehearsed. He had little patience for such rants and saw no further need for this discussion. "If, during their time there, they continue to seek forgiveness, they will find it. We established both our Kingdom and Turayn under Free Will, though the similarities between the two essentially end there."

"But, isn't Free Will what got us here in the first place?" Magnor blunted out in a final attempt to offer his disapproval. He had taken a seat next to the hearth and also seemed to be settling in comfortably.

"Yes, Free Will is what got us here," said Carasi who was becoming increasingly annoyed. "Free Will allowed Patho to make his departure and take so many with him. And, it will be Free Will that allows the Fallen Souls to find redemption. Now, enough talking, the day has come to an end." Carasi took the lead toward the door. Grabbing Ferrul by the arm he said, "Let's get out of here now. No more discussion!" With that, the two left the room.

"Well, I guess that's all then?" Konnory said with a laugh. Konnory looked around the room in hopes of finding someone with whom he could continue the discussion. Jael was back to his reading and Father had made it clear that a debate between he and Magnor was not on the evenings agenda. Giving into the understanding that the evening was truly coming to an end, he stood and made his way to the door. "Are you coming, Jael?" he shouted back. "Oh, never-mind. You have your nightly reading to do, don't you?" Without turning around, Konnory took his leave.

As the door closed, Magnor looked over to the King, "What's he talking about?" he asked.

"Jael stops to read any additional requests from the Fallen Souls received from the day," The King answered.

"There are more than what he is currently reading? Do they come in all day long?" asked Magnor.

"Sometimes," Jael responded, as he began collecting the requests spread out in front of him.

"Most of the time," the King corrected.

Jael stood and, with a stack of requests in hand, made his way to the door. "Good night, Father, and thank you," Jael said as he pushed the doors open. The King nodded and with a warm smile said good night.

Magnor sat for a moment. With no one left but Father to debate, he, too, decided the day had come to an end. He rose from his seat, made his way to the table to deposit his now empty goblet and walked to the door. "You are sure about this?" Magnor asked, turning to his Father.

"I am sure," the King said. "And you will be, too, someday."

"We'll see," Magnor saluted the King as he made his exit.

The King sat in the empty and quiet room. He was confident this was right. He was also saddened by the fact that it was necessary.

A servant entered the room. Seeing the King, he hesitated. "I'm sorry my Lord, I thought you had joined the Princes. Would you like for me to come back after you've retired?"

"No, continue with your duties," responded the King.

The servant walked over to the serving table. He could not ignore the stillness in the room. "Is there anything I can get for you?" the servant asked.

"No, thank you." The King was quiet as the servant began to move around the room. Uncertain if it was wise to continue the conversation, he moved with great hesitance. After a long silence, the King said, "Tomorrow is the beginning of a journey that no one ever thought would be necessary." His words made the hair on the servant's arm stand on end. He felt a chill rise from the floor. The King finished the last few bites of bread and cheese remaining on his plate. He reached for his goblet and sat gazing toward the windows.

The servant continued working, collecting the last of the serving pieces from the table. As he reached for the empty serving pieces closest to the King, he uttered, "Will it be successful,

Sire?" The words seem to escape his lips; it wasn't his place to be conversing in such a manner with the King.

Unbothered by the source of the question, the King took a sip of wine and gently nodded his head. "Yes. Unfortunately...it will."

The King's tone made the servant's heart sink. He had never witnessed such a state of vulnerability from his King. "Unfortunately?" he asked. Forgetting his tasks as this rare privilege of discussion with his King presented itself.

"Yes," the King repeated. He took another sip of wine. He looked up at the servant, "The price that will be paid," The King closed his eyes and shook his head, "such an enormous price."

The servant didn't move. He wanted to, but his feet felt glued to the floor. With only a sliver of hope in his voice, he asked, "Sire, will it be worth it?"

The King sat motionless. Finally, he took a deep breath. His eyes wandered into space. As he shook his head, he replied, "Let us hope so, my friend. Let us hope so."

Chapter Four

When the morning of the great adventure arrived, the King and the Princes made their final preparations for their journey. Ferrul assured them that sufficient supplies had been sent on ahead. The royal chariots had been prepared, the horses groomed and brought to the front entrance of the castle.

The King and Queen waited for the Princes. Arm in arm they stood at the entrance. The castle was a scurry of activity as all were doing their final check for departure. Carasi and Ferrul were the first to make an appearance.

"Of course, they would be the first," the Queen chuckled as she squeezed the King's arm.

"Would you have expected anything else?" the King laughed.

Jael and Konnory appeared a short time later. Jael was aglow. "His feet are barely touching the ground," the Queen whispered. "He has great expectation."

"Indeed, he does," said the King. "This is his doing."

"Not all of it," she replied. "He's just the one..."

"Get a move on!" Jael yelled back to the trailing Magnor. "You're never late. We're doing this with or without you."

"Father overruled us and said you had to come," Konnory added.

"I'm coming! I'm coming!" replied Magnor making his way down the corridor. "As if the rest of eternity can't wait a moment longer!" he muttered.

The Queen took the King's hand, "They would be lost without you!"

"I sincerely doubt that," He replied. "These five have proven, not only their great intelligence these past months, but also their diligence and integrity. I'm very proud of our boys."

Jael stopped to greet Mother. Leaning over, he kissed her on the cheek. "Good-bye Mother. No doubt everything will be well under control in our absence."

"You jest - right? Everything will run better in our absence," Konnory remarked. Following Jael, he gave Mother a kiss. "Have fun!" he said, as he headed toward the chariots.

Magnor stopped and faced her, "Are you sure you don't need me to stay behind?"

The Queen smiled and her nose crinkled. "I love you for asking, but I'm not entirely sure it's a selfless offer."

"She will be fine," the King assured.

"No doubt, no doubt at all. Just checking," Magnor leaned in and said, "Good-bye Mother, I'll keep them in line."

"I'm sure you'll try," she said, putting her hand on his cheek.

Magnor walked to the line of chariots with all the authority of the Commander of the King's Army. He made his way to the King's chariot and took the reigns. The King climbed aboard and settled in behind him. It was only in recent times that the King allowed Magnor to drive his chariot. He now took great pride in riding behind his son. Allowing Magnor to have the reins was not a threat; it was a sign of strength. Jael escorted Ferrul in the second chariot as Carasi and Konnory claimed the last.

As the whips snapped in the air, the horses sped off leaving the castle in a cloud of dust. The journey took them through the gardens. They were perfectly tended, lush, and full of color. The gardens spread out for miles. As they made their way past, the gardeners and servants bowed low.

Outside of the castle proper they began to make their way into the hillsides. There was something majestic in the beauty of the Kingdom. It was perfection. It was all the Princes had ever known, and all they cared to know. The journey took them through a few villages and towns. There had been such commotion the day before as the transport units passed through, making it impossible to keep the King and the Princes' journey a secret. The King's subjects took full advantage of any opportunity to honor their King. Awaiting their arrival at each place was a welcome from the entire village; banners unfurled in the wind, flower petals lined the streets. As the King's procession entered, the cheers could be heard to the next town. As the King passed, each villager bowed low.

There was no one remaining in the Kingdom that had any desire to leave. Not since the day Patho made his exit. There were those that had considered leaving with him, but had a change of mind before stepping out of the Kingdom gates. Those that remained found a deeper sense of gratitude and respect for their King. They loved him and wanted to honor him in everything they did.

As the convoy approached the outer region, they could see in the distance the camp that would be their home for the next six days. A large pavilion had been erected in the center surrounded by a multitude of smaller tents. As always, Carasi and Ferrul left no detail to chance.

The royal travelers were greeted upon their arrival. Each was escorted to their personal dwelling to settle in and get refreshed before meeting for nourishment. The horses were taken to their temporary stables. After settling into their tents, the men gathered for a meal before they began their excursion to the edge of the Kingdom.

The six were unaccompanied as they made the final leg. They would journey to the edge of the Kingdom on foot. All five Princes had been trained as warriors and during their training had all spent time on the outer edges of the Kingdom. Those visits brought a sense of adventure and discovery of the unknown. This visit was different. The vast Darkness no long represented emptiness, it was now inhabited by the Fallen Souls. It had become a symbol of separation from the King. Each one was sobered by the realization that it was now home to many they loved. As they grew closer and closer to the edge, their hearts grew heavy.

The King stood peering out. Behind him laid his magnificent Kingdom; before him was the Darkness. He stood silently. His sons circled in around him. There was a quiet boldness that surrounded the six men. Those watching from the camp knew they were witnessing an event of unmatched importance. The Plan in its entirety was only known to the Royal Family, but those who watched from a distance, watched with great anticipation.

Ferrul stood on one side of the King prepared with the files and blueprints. There was to be established a new realm called Turayn. This would be the place the Fallen Souls would be allowed to inhabit. Turayn would be their entrance back into the Kingdom.

Jael stood to the King's left. His heart raced as he looked out into the Darkness. This was their chance. Turayn would make it possible for any who had left to come home. His brothers, Quaine and Palti, could be close by. He would do anything to make a way for them to return.

The King motioned with his right hand to an area that lay just outside the Kingdom, "This is where we will establish Turayn."

"So close?" questioned Konnory. "I didn't realize it would be that near to the Kingdom."

"Yes," Ferrul said. "It will allow for stronger protection. Those who will volunteer to stand guard will be in Patho's territory as they surround Turayn. The close proximity to the Kingdom allows us to change the guard with as little disruption as possible. It also allows for close observation from within the Kingdom."

Magnor rolled his eyes. "Perhaps we should hope that Patho spends all his time attacking the regiments and leaves Turayn alone."

"For what purpose?" asked Carasi.

"Then my troops and I could take care of him once and for all!" Magnor raised his eyebrows hoping to sell the idea.

"Yes, that's exactly what we need. You are always the warrior aren't you?" Ferrul shook his head and continued, "If by chance, there are those who are successful in seeking forgiveness..."

"By chance?" Jael repeated. "This is not going to be by chance. They will come. I know they will!"

"Either way, Father desires that they are as close to the Kingdom as possible. We are unsure of what the effects of such a degree of repentance could create. Having them close may assist in drawing them back to us."

"Degree of Repentance?" questioned Magnor.

"Yes," replied Ferrul. "Not the degree from each individual, but rather the possible effect of so many seeking forgiveness at the same time. We have not witnessed it in such a degree as is possible in Turayn. It is one of the unpredictable variables in The Plan."

"Do you really think there could be a negative effect?" Konnory asked.

"We can't be sure," Carasi answered. "It's totally unpredictable. The giving and receiving of Forgiveness creates an energy level like no other action we have ever witnessed. Multiply that times the number of Fallen Souls seeking to receive it, we won't know until we have actual data."

"You make it sound like an experiment," Jael said.

"In many ways it is, my brother. We all know you have high hopes and great expectations for the outcome of The Plan, but all of it is untested. We are creating a new world, new territory, new creations."
"Ferrul, are you ready with the blueprints?" questioned the King.

"Yes, Father. All is in order. Are you ready to begin?" Ferrul asked.

The King placed both his hands on Jael's shoulders, they locked eyes. "Are you certain this is what you want?" Jael nodded. The King asked again, "You are certain?" Again, Jael nodded. "Then let us begin. Ferrul, let me see the blueprints."

Ferrul handed the stack of files to Carasi. He opened a file and pulled out the first page.

There had only been one other time that the King considered establishing anything outside the Kingdom. When he first realized that Patho was growing restless, the King gave instructions for a Pit to be created. The Pit provided a place where Patho could be secured away if he became uncontrollable.

The Pit was designed as a large chamber that, once sealed, could not be entered or exited. It contained no windows and it had only one entrance. Crafted from the strongest material available, the chamber would allow nothing, or no one, to enter or exit when sealed. With great deliberation, the King personally selected five of his most trusted warriors to move the chamber out into the Darkness. There were only six who knew of its location. When Patho left the Kingdom, he happened upon the chamber and claimed it as his new headquarters for himself and his warlords. It amused the King when word was sent back that Patho had found the Pit on his own. The King was never surprised by Patho's predictability and arrogance.

Chapter Five

W e must first create the boundary by separating the Darkness," Carasi instructed.

With the blueprints carefully spread out in front of him, the King began to call what had never existed into existence. The sons knew their Father well; nothing would be done out of order. The Plan had been carefully drawn up, and executing it would be done with precision.

The King stretched out his hands and spoke in what was an almost inaudible voice to those in attendance. As the words passed over his lips and out into the vast Darkness, they gained momentum, rolling into waves of energy and sound. They echoed through the Darkness and resounded back across the Kingdom. With the first command, there was such a charge of energy it was felt to the ends of the existence.

"I bet they felt that in the Pit," Konnory said.

"In the Pit? Odds are it will be heard through eternity!" Konnory said.

They watched as the Darkness swirled into motion as if being drawn into the words of the King; mixing together, blending substance with direction. They watched as form began to take shape and a new world began to be established.

Ferrul turned to Magnor, "Send them out," he instructed.

Magnor turned to the captain who stood at attention halfway between the camp and the edge of the Kingdom. Magnor saluted and with a nod, the captain turned toward the camp and blew his horn. The Princes and King watched an army of warriors make their way from the camp to the edge of the Kingdom. These were the first to be trained extensively and exclusively to protect Turayn. As the warriors passed, they saluted their King and then, without hesitation, stepped out into the Darkness.

The Darkness held great mystery. No one from the Kingdom had ever spent any length of time there. The soldiers were risking life itself to protect the new world. The Royals felt the weight of responsibility they carried for each of these warriors.

From the edge of the Kingdom, they stood looking at this new world. The troops making their way around its perimeter. Once in place, they stood at attention guarding this new creation called Turayn. They were ready and determined to protect it no matter what powers may come. They couldn't help but wonder if the Fallen Souls could feel its existence? Had they witnessed its establishing? Could they feel its energy?

As the last of the warriors took their position, the King and his sons returned to camp. There was a great deal more work ahead and countless details to come. Today, the Darkness was no longer completely void. The beginning of hope existed.

On Day Two, the King spoke into existence the atmosphere that would surround and contain Turayn. And on the third day, dry land was given boundaries, establishing the large bodies of water. Upon the dry land, vegetation began to grow, trees filling the hillsides and grass covering the fields.

The Plan stated that day four would be the last day the King could call into existence new creations. From that time forward, all creations were to be created from what already existed. On the fourth day, the sun and moon were established. This separated Turayn from the true Kingdom for it would exist on it own. The Sun and Moon were needed to keep Turayn warm, to ensure the large bodies of water would stay within their boundaries, they provided a day and night for Turayn. The true Kingdom had no such thing. There was day and night, but they were not controlled by a sun and moon; they just were. The true Kingdom was light. It was established this way from the beginning of time.

As evening approached, the King and Princes would make their way back to the camp that had been prepared for them. Dinner was served in the large pavilion, and the evening discussions took place around the fire. Each night they recalled the events of the day and confirmed that preparations were ready for the next.

On the fifth day, the creatures that would live in the water, and those that would fly through the air, would be created. Animals were an important part of the original outline of The Plan. They were needed for nourishment and labor and would assure that life on Turayn was self-sustaining. They would also be an important element in the practice of sacrifice for those seeking forgiveness.

None of them would forget the night these creatures began being designed. Konnory was charged with the task of the original drawings. As he sat contemplating the endless possibilities of creating, Magnor walked into the room.

"What are all those?" Magnor inquired, as he made his way around the table looking at what seemed to be hundreds of drawings.

"The creatures for Turayn," Konnory replied through a yawn and stretching his arms over his head.

"But I thought there were just a few? You must have a hundred drawings."

"I know. I know," Konnory said with arms still stretched in the air. "I started with one or two and then realized that by changing just a few characteristics, the possibilities are endless." Konnory picked up a few of the drawings and continued. "See, just by changing the length of the neck and legs, this becomes an entirely new creature." Pointing to another group of drawings he continued, "And by lengthening the nose on that one, this one is created." Magnor stood comparing the two drawings.

Eventually, he pulled the chair out next to Konnory and sat down. He poured himself some wine and began looking at Konnory's other drawings. It was morning when the others found them still at the table.

"What are you boys so engrossed in?" questioned the King after entering the Dining Room.

His voice startled them, failing to realize they had been working all night. Magnor responded, "Konnory's working on the creatures for Turayn."

"Konnory's working on it? Looks to me like you both are working," said the King.

"I thought we had decided on only a handful of species? There are hundreds of drawings here," said Carasi ,as he slid a chair to Konnory's side.

The King watched as Jael and Ferrul also included themselves in the process. The Princes were so engrossed in their activity, they hadn't noticed the Queen enter the room. She walked behind each of her sons ,as she made her way over to where the King stood. "It appears to be going as you had anticipated," she said quietly. The King chuckled.

It took only moments for Ferrul and Carasi to calculate what effect the addition of so many different creatures would have on Turayn, therefore making the necessary revisions. By the time breakfast was served, there was no space left on the table to set the food.

Jael and Magnor took the large sea creatures. Ferrul was responsible for the small ones, due to their amount of detail. Once Ferrul had begun designing the details of the small sea creatures, he couldn't stop. He became obsessed with the smallest organisms that would inhabit the water. Carasi and Konnory were responsible for designing the birds of the air; following closely the design of the fowl that was found in the Kingdom. At some point, it had become a competition between the two who could bring the most color into one species.

Jael and Magnor found great pleasure in designing their creatures. Their finished designs were oversized and awkward creatures. To everyone's surprise, Magnor was the most entertaining to watch. His creatures were massive beings with very little form.

"How is that going to swim?" Ferrul had asked, as he examined a drawing of what appeared to be a massive fish.

"What's it going to take to feed that thing?" Carasi questioned.

"And you're certain it isn't technically a fish?" Ferrul asked. Jael and Magnor just laughed and moved to the next.

Each species had two designs, a male and female. Jael and Magnor seemed to challenge each other on just how unique they could make each pair. As usual, Magnor had to go to the extreme. He not only created some of the largest and most unique creatures, he also explored ways for them to interact. While drawing one of the largest beasts of the sea, Magnor decided it should depend on one of the smallest creatures for its food. Ferrul couldn't help but feel he was only creating the menu for Jael and Magnor's creatures to eat.

There were several sketches the King had not approved, forcing Magnor to redesign them. There was one ,however, that Magnor somehow convinced the King to approve. How he did it, the brothers could never figure out.

"That one looks as if he combined parts of ten different creatures," Carasi had said.

"I'm not sure if it should live on land or in the water," said the King.

"Is it a bird with no wings?" Ferrul asked. No one was sure what it would eat. With great reluctance the King gave his approval, but he promised it would be the last questionable creature he would approve.

On the fifth day, the Princes would be required to venture to Turayn. Magnor was the only one of them who had ever journeyed out into the Darkness; it had been required as part of his training. The other four brothers had only experienced the Darkness from within the safety and security of the Kingdom. Today, that would change. Magnor would lead the group, but these six were not to make the journey alone.

In the Kingdom there existed a group of beings known as the Messengers. The King had created the Messengers to assist in building the Kingdom. They existed in everyone's earliest memories. They had one purpose and one purpose only, to serve the King. They took their orders directly from him and did as they were told. The Princes knew of them from the time they were children; yet their presence was difficult to understand. When Patho made his exit, the King arranged for the Messengers to make regular trips out into the Darkness. These were the ones who brought the requests for forgiveness back to the Kingdom. These would be the ones who would escort this band of brothers on this day's journey. There was great excitement, anticipation and caution as they began their day.

As the group gathered for breakfast that morning, most were too excited to eat. Even Magnor showed signs of anticipation. The King was amused by their boyish enthusiasm. It only took two words, "Shall we?" for the group to jump to their feet and bound toward the edge of the Kingdom. There awaiting them, was a large regiment of Messengers. They were magnificent to behold. The Princes had only known of their existence, today they saw them. The King took the lead, the five following close behind. The Messengers surrounded them; Magnor assumed they were four or five deep, but he could not tell for sure. He was certain, however, that neither he nor any of his brothers had felt so protected – they had never needed protection.

They were filled with mixed emotions as they entered Turayn. In many ways, it looked so similar to the Kingdom, but they could feel how much more frail it was. The King designated the place where the day's tasks would be completed.

Carasi delivered the drawings to each of their proposed creator. As the Princes were now bringing to life these figures they had designed, the King watched and lightly jested as he inspected their work. It would have been much easier for the King to have simply called into existence each creature, but that is not how Turayn was designed. This place must be self-sustaining; thus everything created that would live in Turayn must come from Turayn and when its lifetime ends, must return to Turayn. Each of the creatures began as sculptures. Upon the King's approval, the creatures were given life and sent to roam Turayn. The men worked tirelessly. That night, the conversation at dinner was filled with discussion of their favorite creations and they joked about the creatures that were yet to come.

Day six mirrored day five. Each Prince took his assigned blueprints and began to create the animals that would inhabit Turayn. As each new creature was completed, the King was called for his approval.

The King had created a secluded garden in Turayn. It resembled his favorite garden outside of the castle in the Kingdom: lush vegetation and gentle flowing streams that cascaded over rocks. It had several purposes. It was a practice kingdom, per se. The first purpose was to allow the King to observe the evolution of his creation. As vegetation grew and spread across Turayn, it would have to adapt to its ever changing surroundings. As creatures would begin to migrate to new regions of Turayn, they too, would have to change, allowing them to survive. The second was to provide a protected place where the beings who housed the Fallen Souls, would have time to understand the workings of Turayn. But the third and most important purpose was to initiate The Plan.

The King created only one creature himself: the vessel that would house the Fallen Souls. It would be called the Human. The King patiently followed every step of the blueprint. He put great care and attention to each detail; it was as if he were creating one of his own. As with the rest of the creatures, the Human must come from Turayn. However, when the figure was completed, it was not given life - that time was yet to come. The King assigned two guards to stand watch over the figure until the appropriate time.

The Princes cherished the days they spent with the King. They found restored levels of energy from seeing the new creations. There had been such a void left in the Kingdom when Patho's plot had been carried out. There had also been little hope of ever bridging that void. But today, they were standing on the edge of what could be great possibility.

For six days these five sons had been at their Father's side. They had watched as Ferrul unfolded the blueprints for that day's work. They had seen Turayn begin to change. Creation was complete. The stage was set for The Plan to begin.

As the morning light welcomed day seven, the Princes began preparing for their journey back to the castle. In the distance, they saw what appeared to be a transport approaching. As it came closer, it grew larger than what they were expecting, or for that matter, what was required. The King joined the spectators.

"Father, I'm afraid we have mixed communications. This is not what was ordered for today," Ferrul offered.

"It may not be what you ordered, but it is what I expected," the King said. As the transport approached, the morning light was reflecting in such a way that it radiated out into the Darkness.

"Father, what have you done?" questioned Carasi.

"These past six days, we have established and put into motion a set of systems to govern over this new universe. There now exists measurements of time different than that of the Kingdom; the sun, moon and stars are placed in such a manner that forces this new universe to operate on its own; those who inhabit this kingdom will experience life and death. Today, I have established one final law; on the seventh day of each week all must rest. Today, we rest and celebrate this new creation. Today, we rest and enjoy each other's company. Today, we rest, for we do not know what tomorrow will bring."

As the transport drew closer, it was apparent the King had prepared for a celebration. Silver and gold serving pieces, and the finest food and wine brought from the King's private reserves. And, of course, there were musicians. Music was essential to any of the King's celebrations.

The King smiled as he watched the caravan approach. Then, suddenly something caught his attention. "Who is leading the procession?" the King asked.

"You don't know?" Ferrul asked. The King shook his head. "She still surprises you, doesn't she?" Ferrul gave the King a loving pat on the arm.

A smile began to grow upon the King's face. His eyes twinkled in delight, "Yes, my Queen still surprises me," the King said with the most gentle, sincere and loving laugh.

After greeting their Mother and helping to unload the chariots, the Princes settled in for a day of feasting. As always, the King was simply delighted in delighting his sons. The seventh day was created for joy.

Outside the Kingdom lay infinite desolation engulfed by blinding darkness. This area had become home to those who had chosen to leave the King's protection. It was impossible to measure the void that filled the Fallen Souls. Nothingness brings such great suffering. Most were consumed by the guilt of leaving the Kingdom. This guilt, mixed with the realization of what they had left, bound them to an eternity of immeasurable anguish.

Patho had established his inner circle. It was made up of those who were in attendance at the first meeting in the Kingdom, as well as a few he had met once outside the gates. There were some that had previously left the Kingdom, and once Patho's departure was realized, joined forces with him.

As a means of disrespect for the King, Patho changed the names of his warlords. He could not have leaders with names from the Kingdom. That would never do! He demanded names that represented his intent. Patho referred to himself as the Highest. He hated the name King. He hated everything about it, including the One who held the title. Patho's Head Advisor was formally known as Wafia meaning "loyal." Patho gave him the name Abaddon, which means "destruction," Loyal Destruction – it was an ideal combination. It was Abaddon's responsibility to make regular reports to Patho on the state of the Fallen Souls. This required Abaddon to spend most of his time traveling the vast Darkness, reporting back his findings.

Letters from the Pit

To Patho, our great leader;

There is still very little to report. The souls that you so brilliantly led away from the kingdom continue to wander aimlessly. They remain lost, confused and hopeless; one could almost feel sorry for them. We still do not know exactly how many followed your successful escape from the confines of the king's control, but it is quite clear that you have won.

Your servant,

Abaddon

To Abaddon,

as there ever any doubt that I would defeat the king
and claim victory? Do not waste your time pitying
the souls. If they were of any use, they wouldn't be out there
wandering around like little lost children; too simple and
weak to quit sniveling and be a part of my glory. It would not
surprise me at all if many more chose to follow the path I laid
out of the kingdom. Hopefully, there will be less futility among
the next wave.

Once again, you have not disappointed me. There may be a
few more battles to fight, but we will indeed win.

The Highest,

Patho

To Patho, our great Victor,

I have heard reports of some activity just outside the kingdom. The information has been vague so I will be making my way there shortly to see it firsthand. It may likely be the next wave of refugees that you spoke of. I will send word as quickly as possible.

Whatever it is, I am certain that you will be able to use it to your benefit.

Your servant,

Abaddon

Chapter Six

There was never any doubt that Turayn, like the Kingdom, would operate under the Law of Free Will. In addition, the Plan's soul purpose was to establish the Law of Forgiveness. It stated that any Human seeking forgiveness through sacrifice would find it. In order to protect both of these Laws, the King would need to hand over total control of the affairs of Turayn to the Humans. The final law, the one that would protect Turayn from being controlled by either the Kingdom or the Pit was called Law of Prevalence. This was essential to assure Turayn remained a neutral place.

The Law of Prevalence:

    1.The legal authority over Turayn belongs to the Human Souls.

    2.There can be no influence or intervention without specific request by a Human.

    3.All are subject to the law.

Any violation of the Law of Prevalence would result in immediate and permanent exile. If Patho violated these laws, he would be sealed into the Pit. If the King violated them, He would be cast from the Kingdom and join the Fallen Souls, leaving the Kingdom open for invasion. There would be no exception. The Laws had been written, sealed by the King and delivered to Patho. Patho knew he would be subject to the Law, unless he found a way around it. Patho was always looking for loopholes in every situation.

Enough time had passed since the six days of creations to observe the evolution of Turayn. There had been several cycles of the seasons. Vegetation flourished, and the creatures had multiplied. From all outward appearance, all was working as intended.

The form the King himself created would be the vessel that housed the Fallen Souls. Unlike life in the Kingdom, life span in Turayn would have an end. The human from would not live forever. It had, after all, only two purposes; to house the Fallen Souls and to breed, creating new life which would provide an endless supply of vessels for the Fallen Souls to inhabit.

Within its frail exterior, the human form held three powerful forces: The mind to create, The heart to feel, and the soul to guide. It would be from these three forces that the Fallen Souls would experience their new life. It would be from these three forces that they would find their way back to the Kingdom.

Out of the dust of the ground, the King had formed the first Human. The first was to be the male vessel. This one, however, would not contain a Fallen Soul. It was necessary for this vessel to allow someone from the Kingdom to enter Turayn. They could not risk the first Fallen Soul to inhabit the human figure untested.

As the King, Carasi and Ferrul sat at the end of the table looking over the final design, the King asked, "Who do we send as the first Human?"

Picking up the final drawing and scanning it intensely, Carasi said, "We'll need someone who is well scripted in The Plan; someone who has a true understanding of the workings of Turayn, someone who is self-sufficient."

"Turayn will be guarded continually," added Magnor. "Besides the warriors, there will be Messengers and Watchers. In case a situation arises that the Watchers are unable to handle, my troops will be close by. The threat of any danger is very low."

Konnory sat at the opposite end of the table. He had been just as much a part of the planning as any of his brothers. He had spent time considering the possible dangers in such a mission. "Father, I would be willing to go," he offered.

The King continued talking, "I will be making regular visits. In fact, I will be there a great deal of time in the beginning. You are correct Magnor, there will be no lack of protection."

Konnory looked at Magnor and then back at the King. Unsure why his first offer wasn't acknowledged, he again nominated himself, "Father, send me."

"Turayn should be self-sufficient," the King said with no hesitation. "We need someone with great communication skills; someone who will be able to teach the Humans about the workings of Turayn. He will have to teach them about sacrifice..."

Konnory looked at Ferrul and then back to Father. Did he not hear me? he thought.

"It must be someone with great wisdom and intellect," continued the King. "One who understands the importance of Free Will and is able to instill its concept in the Humans. More importantly, it must be someone who will ensure that The Plan is initiated."

Konnory pushed his chair back and stood to his feet. "Has no one heard me?" he questioned. "I've offered twice already! I will go!"

The King stared at Konnory. It felt as if he was looking straight through him. No one moved. Then with a hearty laugh the King said, "I heard you the first time! I had to make sure you were serious. I know that after answering three times, one is certain of what they mean. We were hoping you would offer. We can't think of a better, more qualified individual for the job."

"We?" Konnory asked.

"Actually, it was your Mother's suggestion. I couldn't have agreed more," said the King.

"And besides, it gets you out of here for the next...hmmm... umpteen hundred years!" said Magnor.

"That would be your Mother's only reservation," said the King.

It had been unanimous. No one could think of sending anyone else. Konnory would have much to learn. There were still aspects of the human life that were not only unexplored, but also untested. Carasi and Ferrul would be his tutors. The three spent much time in preparing Konnory for his transition.

There was one final trip to be made to Turayn. As the six made their last journey together, they were sobered by the reality of Konnory's future. When they entered Turayn, they couldn't help but notice its evolution. Color spread across its vastness. Creatures roamed in large packs. Life had begun.

They entered the secluded garden. The King dismissed the guards who had been assigned to the lifeless human figures since the day of its creation.

The King was surrounded by his sons: Konnory on His left and Jael on his right. Turning to Konnory, he asked, "My son, today you begin a journey that is essential for the future success of The Plan. You're willingness and eagerness to perform such an act is a reflection of your strength, integrity and wisdom. Magnor will stand watch with his captains to ensure your safety not only in Turayn, but also your safe return to us." The King kissed Konnory on both cheeks. Magnor walked behind Konnory and placed his hand on his shoulder.

The King then turned to Jael. "Son, let it be witnessed today that I, the King, am giving you my authority to bring this plan to an end." Carasi and Ferrul looked at each other in disbelief.

Neither saw this coming. Father had insisted that he have this authority. His insistence bordered on demanding. *Why was he handing it to Jael? What was Father preparing him for?*

The King continued, "I am ordering Magnor to establish a new regiment, larger than has ever existed. Upon your word, they will act - bringing The Plan to an end."

Father's voice echoed in Magnor's head. We have never discussed this, he thought. Why does Jael possess this authority? Why would this not be a collective decision? Why is this the first we've heard...

"Jael, it is because of your determination that I have entertained the thought of such an endeavor. Let it be known that I, the King, am freely handing over my authority in this matter to you. I freely, yet reluctantly, relinquish my power to bring The Plan to an end. And now, I must ask, for the last time, are you certain this is what you desire?"

"Yes Father, it is." Jael said with more certainty than he had ever spoken. They embraced and with a kiss on each cheek, the King turned back to the human figure.

Kneeling next to him, the King was face to face with the lifeless form. The King inhaled and then covering the intended air passages with his mouth, He breathed out, filling the lifeless form with life. At that moment, Magnor's hand fell to his side as Konnory no longer existed in form. Konnory had become a Human.

The human Konnory resided in the secluded garden with the King always close by. It took time for Konnory to feel comfortable in his new skin. He knew of its design. He was there when the King made it. But before he had taken residence, it had only been a design. Now, it was sustaining life.

The human form was so limiting. For the first time, he was aware of sound frequencies. Sound traveled through small channels on opposite sides of his head. In the Kingdom, sound was absorbed through your entire being. His physical form grew tired. He felt hunger. His vision was limited as if he was constantly looking through a goblet.

To his great sadness, he could no longer see Father in his true form. Konnory could only sense his spirit. The King could not make himself visible in Turayn; nothing there could sustain his true presence. If his foot were to touch the ground, the foundations of this new world would crumble. The King's presence was so strong that at times, just being in his presence seemed more than this new human figure could handle.

During their visits, the King and Konnory discussed the growing cycles of the vegetation. They laughed at the uniqueness of the creatures and the strange characteristics Magnor had insisted upon for his animals. They talked about the imperfections of the human form. The King saw a side of Konnory that was so frequently overshadowed by his brothers. He saw Konnory's depth of wisdom and insight. He appreciated his desire to understand a concept from all sides. Konnory was unlike any of his brothers. As each day passed, the King's love for all of his sons grew deeper and deeper. Magnor, too made, frequent visits but they were unobserved. He had always and would always be the protector of his brothers.

After all were sure Konnory had become acclimated to his new life, the King put the male Human into a deep sleep. From his side, he removed a bone, and from that bone, he created a female called woman. The King breathed his breath into her nostrils. They watched as the lifeless form became a vessel for the first Fallen Soul. They wanted desperately to know who, and for that matter, how this first Fallen Soul had been chosen. But that was not for them to know. A Fallen Soul's identity would be known only once they were welcomed back into the Kingdom.

Witnessing The Plan come to life was more electrifying than any of them had anticipated. They were watching first hand all of their planning, all of the preparation literally - coming to life.

The two Humans shared the beauty of the King's Garden. They learned to tend the vegetation and care for the animals. Konnory and the woman enjoyed every moment of every day. All they needed was provided. They were safe within the boundaries of the Garden.

They all knew Patho had an essential part to play in The Plan. Unbeknown to him, his participation would be the key that opened the only way back to the Kingdom. Patho was deceitful, cunning and manipulative. What he wasn't - was insightful. He could not see the future. The King needed to get his attention once again. The King had deliberately done so twice in the past. The feasting and celebrating they had done after the creation of Turayn had been a way to make noise and pique Patho's interest. When the Laws were delivered to the Pit, it was not only to inform him of the Laws and their consequences, it was also to make sure he was aware of Turayn. The time that Konnory and the woman spent in the garden was not only for their benefit, but also to provide time needed to ensure Patho's participation.

To our conqueror, Patho

I have made my way to the location where the reports were coming. It appears the king has created a miniature version of the kingdom. Is it possible he is admitting defeat and has made a sanctuary for the few faithful that remain? I plan to make a closer inspection soon provided you feel it is necessary.

Your servant,

Abaddon

Abaddon,

A sanctuary? Of course, it is possible the king is finally coming to terms with his inferiority. Inspect closer and report back to me immediately. I received a sealed set of Laws from the imbecile. He is clearly grasping at straws trying to assert authority over his sanctuary; which is apparently called Turayn.

I expect your report shortly after this message leaves my hands.

The Highest,

Patho

To our great subjugator, Patho

I have examined Turayn. It is covered by many different types of plants and creatures. After seeing but a few of the creatures, it is clear that the king is losing his mind. I discovered one particular area that resembles an area near his castle. There are two beings living there, but they also are much smaller than the normal version. Perhaps the king is breeding slaves to care for them when they abandon the kingdom.

Your servant,

Abaddon

Abaddon,

They could be slaves. Or maybe the king is trying to create a new set of subjects to replace the ones I've stolen. It will be difficult not to gloat anytime I think of his tiny sanctuary and tiny subjects. I shall ruin his shameful paradise before it even takes root. Find a way to make the two peons turn against the king before he arrives. Serpent seems to be getting restless, make sure that he has some role to play in whatever is done. I will do all that I can to ensure that disappointment greets the king wherever he goes.

The Highest,

Patho

Chapter Seven

The male and female humans thrived in the Garden. Daily they walked with the King. The three talked, asked questions and simply enjoyed the time together. Konnory settled into his new life. The only dissatisfaction he felt was his inability to see the King.

The Garden had become home to him. In the center of the Garden, the King had created two trees. The Tree of Everlasting Life stood tall and stately, it was like no other. The Tree of Complete Understanding was equally as tall, its branch's bending under the weight of its luscious fruit. Both trees had been unsuspicious, that is until now.

During this particular visit, the King made a point to lead the humans to the center of the garden. He knew of Patho's spies were lurking close by. Konnory was also aware. The King pointed out the stateliness of the Tree of Everlasting Life. As they passed the Tree of Complete Understanding, He stopped and very obviously reminded them they were not allowed to eat from this tree.

Word was sent back to Abaddon and it was the avenue he needed. He quickly made ready for the attack. As Patho suggested, he had charged Serpent to do his bidding. Serpent was an evil soul, the ultimate demon. If he had been in the Kingdom when Patho plotted his escape, Serpent would have been his righthand man. He was a quick thinker. Talked out of both sides of his mouth, usually at the same time. He could change direction in an instant. He never claimed responsibility and never needed to. It didn't matter what anyone thought of him, it only mattered what he thought. He didn't need anyone, he just needed to use them. Patho would have tried to leveraged all these strengths. But it was more likely that if he had been in the Kingdom, Serpent would not have allowed Patho any leverage.

There were those who left the Kingdom before Patho. Serpent had left the Kingdom so long ago that few could even recall his life there. For those who had chosen to live in the Darkness, including Serpent, there was a noticeable change in their appearance. Whether it was from the lack of interaction, or the length of time spent alone in the Darkness, they all became unrecognizable. After coming across a group of them during a surveillance excursion in the Darkness, one of the commanders had referred to them as *Others*. Patho had also come across several Others and had convinced more than a few to join him in the Pit.

Later that same day, after the King's departure, Abaddon summoned Serpent to the Garden. There was no guarantee Serpent would oblige. Abaddon waited. He watched as the female strolled toward the center of the Garden. She sat in the shade of a neighboring tree. Abaddon left himself begin to twitch. A reaction that had just recently begun. He did his best to control it but with no success. Patho was the cause, he knew it. He watched, and twitched, and watched some more. The female sat for awhile and as she began to stand, Abaddon saw him. Serpent was on the move.

The light from the sun illuminated and warmed the human's face as she gazed up. Serpent had been watching from a distance. He had been out of everyone's sight, especially Abaddon's.

"This is quite a magnificent dwelling," he began as he approached.

"Yes," responded the woman, "the King has provided for every need we could possibly have."

"I can see that. He has given you this beautiful place to live, you have all the nourishment you will ever need just waiting to be plucked," Serpent said hanging on to the last word. "You don't have to do a thing." Serpent began to move slowly toward the Tree of Complete Understanding. The woman followed. "And all of this with no restrictions; how ex-cell-ent," he hissed. When he and the woman were standing directly in front of the Tree of Complete Understanding, he stopped. He was delighted that she had followed him so willingly. Serpent spoke slowly as he mingled breath with speech. "And these must be the most delicious fruit in the entire Garden."

"I would not know," she answered.

Continuing is a slow and inquisitive utterance, "What do you mean, you would not know? You haven't tasted it?"

"No, indeed I have not." She shook her head but her eyes did not leave the tree.

"Why ever not?" Serpent asked. He moved closer to the tree, reached out to hold one of its fruits. As he inspected it, making sure the light of day reflected off of it, he said, "Look at it! Surely it must be the finest fruit in the garden." Serpent motioned for the woman to step closer, to his greater delight, she did.

"It is not for us to eat," she simply replied.

"Then who is it here for, the birds?" Serpent asked. He spanned the sky with his glance.

There was great hesitation in the woman's response. She had never pondered this before. If not to provide for them, what was this tree for? "I'm not sure why it is here. The King has instructed us not to eat of it." With each word, the woman became more and more fixated on the fruit hanging in front of her. It never dawned on her to ask who Serpent was or from where he had come. Serpent had effortlessly mesmerized her.

"You must be mistaken. Why would the King give you something so marvelous and then tell you not to touch it?" Serpent made an attempt to be lighthearted and chuckle, at such an idea. Abaddon cringed and made a mental note that *lightheartedness* was never to be attempted again by this one.

"It seems selfish and cruel," Serpent said with a great sigh.

"But he has given us so much..." she said in defense of the King.

Serpent could already sense curiosity and doubt had entered her mind. "This tree—this very tree—has the power to open your mind," Serpent put great emphasis on the word mind. "It will allow you to think like the King!" Serpent dangled the fruit in front of the woman, while he spoke softly in her ear.

"Like the King?" asked the woman.

"Yesssssss!" He was so close to her he could touch her. "To be able to think, ...to reason, ...to live like the Queen! Thisssss the only reason hhhheee has forbidden it! And he de-siresss to have total control over you! Ahhh, but once you partake of this fruit, you can be his equal!"

"His equal?" she asked. She was no longer blinking, Serpent had her in his grip and he knew it.

"Yessss! hisss equal! Take it – eat! As you said, He has given you so much. Why stop there? You may as well have e-v-e-r-y-t-h-i-n-g-!"

Without hesitation, she reached for the fruit. Abaddon watched with intensity. She opened her mouth and his entire body shook. She bit. Serpent hissed. Abaddon sighed. The King moaned as His untainted connection to the humans was broken. Disobedience had entered Turayn and had permanently corrupted the Human Soul. The female shared the fruit with Konnory. With no objection, Konnory ate as well. The Plan was now fully underway.

The King returned that evening to the Garden. There was heaviness in his heart. He knew it was imperative for a separation to happen between He and the inhabitants of Turayn, a separation that would last for a very long time. Knowing didn't make it any easier. The King knew this one act would bring great conflict. He no longer would be able to freely provide the Humans their every need. Their life would now be filled with hard labor. For a short time, life in Turayn was how He desired it to always be; the King providing for his subjects; his subjects living a content, peaceful and gracious life. They would now struggle to survive in Turayn. They would also have to fight their way back to the King. When they did, He would be waiting patiently to welcome them.

Konnory heard the King calling. Something stirred within him. Konnory had heard the King call him many times since he had taken residence in the Garden. His beckoning was always met with great excitement and anticipation. It was not excitement he was feeling. There was apprehension, anxiety, and worst of all, fear. He knew he had nothing to fear; it was Father. This was part of The Plan. Carasi and Ferrul had prepared him for this....

No, he thought, *they told me about this, but none of us could have been prepared for it. None of us has ever experienced this…this separation. Why didn't we see it? How could we have not understood that it was the separation from Father that caused the Fallen Souls to plead for forgiveness?* Konnory was beginning to understand the plight of the Fallen Souls; the vast Darkness, the emptiness and loneliness would no doubt be agonizing. But it must be the separation from Father that was making it unbearable.

Konnory heard Father's call once again. As he turned to take his partner's hand, he realized he was not alone in this torment. He had to force her to look at him. He had never seen such an expression of fear.

"We must go," Konnory said softly.

"We can't face him," she said. "How will we be able to look upon him?"

"I don't know," Konnory replied. "But we must try. He will know. We must trust that He will know."

As Konnory and the woman approached the King, Konnory saw the carcass off to the side. The King was holding two garments made from the skins. "Blood must be shed," Konnory whispered.

Sacrifice, the shedding of blood, was a requirement for forgiveness and he had been well scripted on the topic. That was all it had been - a topic. No different than anything that had been taught in his schooling or discussed at the dinner table. But this was no longer merely a topic; it was a reality. Konnory's human soul was now separated from the King's. A sacrifice would be required to bring them back together. The King had provided the first sacrifice; Konnory would now be responsible to carry on this practice. In doing so, he would be asking for forgiveness.

It was now time for Konnory and the woman to leave the Garden. The King placed guards at its entrance. He surrounded the Garden with a small regiment to prevent anyone from entering or exiting. This beautiful place had served its purpose. If left unguarded, the humans could potentially eat from the Tree of Everlasting Life. In doing so, they would eliminate any hope of redemption.

The King's return to the Kingdom was like none before. The Princes witnessed the pain on his face.

"It is complete," he said, entering the Dining Room. All had underestimated the heaviness this event would bring.

"His life will be very different now," Jael said.

"Yes, the separation has been made," said the King.

"He will now have to labor endlessly for his survival," Carasi said. "We did our best to foresee all that would be entailed in this, but undoubtedly we could not have understood the emotional strain. And ours cannot possibly compare to his."

"How did Patho do it?" Jael asked.

"He sent Serpent to do his bidding," the King replied.

"Serpent?" Magnor asked.

The King had made his way to the end of the table and took his seat. An attendant stepped forward offering him a plate, the King refused. "Serpent left the Kingdom many years ago," began the King. "He's completely indifferent and loyal to no one but himself. He is totally unpredictable and in some ways that makes him more of a threat than Patho." These words made the Princes sit up in their chairs. "Serpent thrives on creating chaos. It matters not to him if it's for the good or evil - as long as he can stir the pot and watch it boil."

"This would have been a prime opportunity for him," Carasi said. "How did he get the woman to eat?"

"He offered her equality," said the King.

"Equality? To what?" Ferrul asked.

"Not to what, to whom," said the King. "Equality to Me."

The group sat quietly. Finally Magnor broke the tension, "And that was enticing?" he asked. The brothers began to laugh. Their laughter eased the King's heaviness.

When the Queen entered the Dining Room, she greeted each of her sons. Then, making her way to the King, she didn't take her eyes off him. She leaned over and kissed his forehead. "Your day was not an easy one," she said gently. The King nodded. "Not easy, but essential. I believe it is now time to inform the Kingdom of The Plan."
There had been great speculation in the Kingdom caused by the commotion made by the King and Princes in establishing

Turayn. Warriors were being trained, not for battle but for protection. Some had returned home to inform family members that they would be gone for long periods of time. They assured their loved ones that all was well but were unable to tell them of their mission. This brought even more questions about the current ongoings in the Kingdom. There was definitely unusual activity at the edge of the Kingdom as well. Camps were set up to house a great number of warriors. The King, himself, had made many journeys there. Konnory had not been seen for some time now, and the Queen was overseeing the business of the Kingdom. Nothing was as it had been.

The Queen was correct, it was time to inform the Kingdom of Turayn. Invitations had been delivered to the leaders of each town and village. The King requested each to send three delegates to the castle. This only heightened the anticipation felt in the Kingdom. On the day of their arrival they were warmly greeted by the King and Queen. Food was set out in the gardens and music played in the background. For those in attendance, this appeared to be a celebration.

Jael had been elected to speak. He was to explain The Plan, its purpose and the recent events in Turayn. After time of introductions and greetings, the group gathered in the center of the garden as Jael began to speak.

"We welcome you here today and are honored to have you in attendance. There have been events recently that have undoubtedly caught your attention," Jael looked across the sea of faces, some with raised brows and some with large smiles, others nodding in agreement. "The activity that you have observed or heard of was the beginning of what we hope will be a way to redemption. The King has created a plan that will offer forgiveness to those who have left the Kingdom." There was a great collective gasp and then everything went quiet. Jael waited a moment, allowing his words to sink in. "It is a plan that will allow those who have left us a way of return." The crowd couldn't believe what they were hearing. No one had anticipated such an announcement. Tears began to flow across the sea of faces.

Each one in attendance was in disbelief. No one had ever considered that this would be possible. They had lived with the heartache of separation. They had felt a loneliness that at times was unbearable. Not knowing where their loved ones were or what was happening to them, caused great pain. Jael was opening the door to hope. Chatter began to break out. "Is it possible?" "How will this happen?" "When will they come home?"

Jael waited and then began to quiet the crowd. "The Plan has been designed to offer forgiveness for anyone seeking it..." Jael then laid out the working of The Plan. He introduced Turayn and told of its creation. He told them of Konnory's willingness to be the first human. He told them about Serpent, about the separation and sacrifice, making it possible for forgiveness to be offered.

"I know you have many questions and will continue to have them," Jael said. "We will do all we can to provide answers. There is one question that we will not be able to answer for you; we do not know who the souls are who inhabit Turayn. We will not know until they return home. But there will be those that will return home." A few cheers were shouted from the crowd. It grew into applause and then into shouts of joy and celebration. As the King, Queen and Princes could no longer be observers, each began to smile, then laugh, as they felt the joy and relief and hope that was spreading across the garden.

It took some time for Jael to gain control once again, but then again, he wasn't putting much effort into it. When he had their attention for the final time, he continued, "In order to provide the opportunity for some to return home, it also means there will be some who may not." A flood of emotions flowed across those in attendance. Jael waited once again. "We have brought you here to spread the word. Go back to your homes, your villages and towns and tell them of The Plan. Spread this hope and joy that you are feeling right now. Although it comes with a great cost, there is finally hope that some will return."

The news spread quickly, and with it, the heaviness and darkness that had shadowed the Kingdom began to leave. Fathers, mothers, brothers, and sisters who had been missing for so long were now able to return. They would all have to wait, but hope is always better than hopelessness.

Letters from the Pit

To our supreme deity, Patho

The mission was a complete success! The Humans, as they are called, were left completely unguarded, and it took no effort at all for Serpent to twist their desires and turn from the king's instructions. The king was so upset, he evicted them from the garden he had built for them! As always, your plan worked perfectly. I plan to resume my usual inspections.

Your servant,

Abaddon

Abaddon,

Do not leave just yet. The king may make more of these Humans, and if they are all as weak-minded as the first two, I'd welcome him to do so. Inform me of any changes and make certain that any new Humans are turned away as well. Continue using the fruit since it worked so well. The less effort it takes, the more it will humiliate the king.

The Highest,

Patho,

About the fruit - for some reason, the tree withered up and the fruit began rotting shortly after the humans ate from it. I don't think it would be very easy to convince it to be eaten anymore.

There is a second tree nearby that the king has posted guards around, but it doesn't seem to have any fruit.

We will find new ways to contaminate them.

Your servant,

Abaddon

Chapter Eight

With each human birth, another Fallen Soul entered Turayn. Upon their arrival, all memory of past life vanished. A short time after leaving the Garden, Konnory became a father, not to just one son but two. As a human father, it was Konnory's responsibility to train his sons in the tasks of everyday life, as well as instructing the two boys on the required practice of sacrifice. Each understood its importance as it related to seeking forgiveness; each knew the King required it. They watched their father offer sacrifice daily from the time they could remember. As they grew, they assisted their father. When Bar and his brother were old enough, they followed this practice. They were diligent in bringing their sacrifices to the King.

On one particular day, the King had shown special appreciation for Bar's sacrifice. This enraged his brother and birthed a deep sense of jealousy within him.

The King confronted Bar's brother directly. "What troubles you so?" he asked.

"You have shown great favor on my brother, but not on me," was his reply.

"My son," the King warned, "be very aware of the emotions that you are allowing to control you."

"Allow?" he questioned. "I have no control over these emotions, these feelings. They come from deep within; they are a part of me. And besides, YOU brought this on."

"You are mistaken," the King said. "You do have control over them. If you do not take that control, they are able to not only control your thoughts but also force you to act. You have the power to change your attitude. If you do, favor will follow you as well. But if you choose not to, you will find it increasingly difficult to control your thoughts and emotions; they will soon control you. You must choose to rule over them."

The King's warning was not heeded. Bar's brother allowed jealousy and anger to take control of him. In the quiet of the afternoon, he found Bar alone in the field and killed him.

Death was an unknown experience to Konnory. The emotions created by the death of his human son were equal to those experienced the day of Patho's departure from the Kingdom. Konnory's only comfort was in knowing that Bar would be returning to the Kingdom. He longed to be there to greet him, to celebrate with the others, to witness the return of the first Fallen Soul.

The celebration was spectacular as Bar returned home. It did not go unnoticed; music, waving banners, and cheers marked Bar's homecoming. The entire Kingdom waited with great anticipation for the possible arrival of those they had lost. Bar's return provided hope that others would also return.

Konnory remained in Turayn for many years. His days were filled with the toils of life and his nights of dreams of the Kingdom. As his time to return to the Kingdom grew closer, a great celebration was planned. The King remained close to Konnory during his final days. As Konnory's human form deteriorated, the King watched until Konnory was breathing his final breaths.

Unlike the Fallen Souls, Konnory had not turned his back on the King; yet in his human form, he did experience separation. It was expected that the Fallen Souls may struggle with accepting forgiveness. They would have to face the choice they had made to leave the King. Their reintroduction into the Kingdom would be a process. Konnory would not face those struggles. Nevertheless, there would be some effect.

The King arranged that Konnory would be escorted to the Garden where it all first began. Still guarded by warriors, the King felt it was the perfect place for their first meeting. He would spend as much time as needed with Konnory until he was ready to return home. The Garden is where the separation had happened; it would be there that the restoration would be completed. The King waited eagerly for Konnory to arrive.

As the human Konnory took his last breath, the kingly Konnory was escorted to the Garden. The King welcomed him with open arms. In his kingdomly self, Konnory could look see his Father's face. This had been a sacrifice that he had not understood fully until his arrival into the human body. Konnory stared into his eyes. He put his hand out and gently laid it on his Father's cheek. How he had longed to see his face, to gaze into his eyes. Konnory breath was slow and deep as he stood face to face with the King. Finally, he allowed himself to be engulfed in the King's embrace. Konnory felt safe in his Father's arms. They both felt the separation beginning to heal. They walked through the Garden, remembering the early days there. They talked of the separation, of sacrifice, and of redemption. It was because of his willingness to be a part of initiating The Plan that this separation occurred; the King wanted to make sure Konnory had time. By that afternoon, the King escorted Konnory back to the Kingdom.

Konnory had requested the King not tell his brothers of his exact return. The King took his leave and met the others in the Dining Room. Konnory would follow shortly.

As Konnory walked through the corridors, he stopped every few feet and took in the details of this magnificent place, every color, and every smell; how could anyone have chosen to leave this? Konnory made his way down the hall. He could see the fire's glow and hear his brothers' banter. This was the one sound he had so dearly missed. As he entered the room, chairs, goblets, and papers went flying as his brothers leapt to their feet to welcome him home.

"Welcome my brother!" Jael was the first to embrace him. With each welcome and embrace, the brothers realized how much they had truly missed him.

"We've been watching and Father has told us of your adventures." Carasi made his way over to the serving table and began preparing a plate for Konnory. "He also kept us updated on the changes you've recommended for the Human."

"Yes, we've been working on a few of your requests already," said Ferrul. "Unfortunately, most of them would create long term effects with unpredictable outcomes." Ferrul put his arms around Konnory's shoulder and led him toward Carasi. "But it is so good to have you home."

"I don't know what we were thinking to leave them there seven, eight, even nine hundred human years!" said Konnory. "Six hundred years in the Kingdom is nothing, but on Turayn - it's an eternity! After putting up with that place for two hundred years - forgiveness should just be offered!"

"You really weren't there that long in Kingdom time," Magnor corrected. And if anyone cares to remember, that's what I said from the beginning!"

"We have taken your advice and shortened the life span," Ferrul added. "Actually, it was your advice and Father's realization that any more than 120 years and the Human became intolerable."

"Present company excluded, of course," said the King.

"It may not have seemed long to you, but I was the one living out every minute. Couldn't you have made that change a few hundred years ago?" Konnory asked.

"I did my best to try to get you back earlier." Magnor boasted. "I made several attempts, believe me. Sorry, I wasn't successful. You could have been home long ago if you weren't so resilient."

Konnory stopped and pondered Magnor's words. He recalled several close calls that almost cost him his life. Consumed with questions, he looked at Magnor. "That was you? How many times?" Magnor nodded and offered a mischievous grin. "I was beginning to think life in Turayn was just abnormally dangerous." Looking at Jael for confirmation.

"Yes, several times," Jael said, nodding in agreement.

Konnory arched his back as if to get a cramp out. He rubbed his forehead and stretched his neck. With furrowed brow, he began to rub his shoulder as though it was still badly injured, "Do you know how long it took me to recover from that tree incident?"

Magnor reached out and grabbed Konnory's shoulder, patting the identified injury several times. With a laugh, he reached for a carafe and goblet. Filling it, he handed it to Konnory. Konnory took a long, slow, sip. He closed his eyes and swallowed ever so slowly. "Nothing like that in Turayn?" jested Magnor.

"No. Nothing even close." Konnory paused and looked around the room. "It's good to be home!" Konnory raised his goblet to his brothers. Each grabbed their goblet and joined him.

"It's great to have you home!" Jael added. "There hasn't been one bit of intelligent conversation since you left. It's been all business, budgets, and battles."

Carasi in a rare moment of not having his nose in a ledger, cheered back, "Consider yourself fortunate we included you in the business, budget, and battle discussions. You would have been very lonely without them."

"There were times I would have done anything to be a part of those conversations. The life there is so mundane. It takes great effort not to spend the day asleep. By the way, which one of you is responsible for designing the Human's need for sleep?" Konnory asked as he enjoyed another sip of wine.

"Yes, we know. Sleeping seems such a waste of time, but the human form requires it. We have seen how it is abused, however. Sleeping was designed as a function, not a pastime," Carasi added.

"The human mind seems to take those things that were designed for utilitarian purposes and make them a luxury. They do it with eating as well!" Konnory said.

"We've noticed," said Ferrul. "I believe that will cause a great deal of problems. When Patho gets wind of that, he'll use it to his full advantage. Tell me, did you enjoy dreaming?"

"Yes, I actually did. Interesting experience. It was almost entertaining," Konnory paused and gazed up to the ceiling, as he remembered the life that already seemed a distant past. "There were nights, however, that were very disturbing. There doesn't seem to be any way to control them." Konnory took his seat at the table. "The human form is so frail. You stumble over a rock or a boulder rolls down a hill and clips your ankle..." he paused and looked inquisitively at Magnor. Magnor grinned and shrugged his shoulders. Shaking his head, he continued, "and it takes forever for the pain to go away - if it ever does. And the lack of strength..." Konnory shook his head again, directing his question to Magnor. "Have you witnessed any battles there? It's amazing anyone can win. It's like watching children out in the field fighting with sticks."

"Yes, I would agree." Magnor laughed and continued. "I've not seen many, but those I have witnessed are quite amusing."

"It's the aging process that is the worst. It's as if all the senses deteriorate before the body does," Konnory continued. "The eyesight begins to fade and then the hearing..."

Jael looked at Konnory and began silently mouthing words.

Konnory stared at Jael for a moment. Jael stared back as if waiting for an answer. Magnor was the first to break the silence with laughter. Carasi simply shook his head. "Very clever, I see you've been working on your delivery while I've been gone. I hope it didn't take all your time. What else have you been working on?" Konnory asked.

The King let out a bellow of laughter as he shifted back into his chair. It had been a long, long time since he sat at the table so comfortably. In the morning, they would leave the castle and join the celebration. For now, the King wanted to enjoy the fact that five of his sons were home. There was no guarantee the others would find their way back, but for today, five was good. It was very good.

"Your Mother is expecting you. She is in the garden," the King said.

Konnory hastily reached for the carafe and refilled his goblet, spilling in his hurriedness. Holding the goblet in one hand, he grabbed a roll with the other and bolted for the door, sending attendants scattering to get out of his way. Turning to push the doors open, he shouted, "See you all later!" Looking at the attendants who were trying to get their balance back, he said, "Oh, sorry about that." And he was gone. As the doors closed, they all heard Konnory's voice shouting, "Mother – I'm BACK!"

The Princes joined the King in his laughter.

Letters from the Pit

To our great ruler, Patho

It appears the king has made the Humans disposable! I was watching two of them today and one just stopped being alive. All it took was one strong bash with a rock from the other. The king must have been in a rush since he didn't even bother to make them very sturdy. And all of this happened simply because one was jealous of the other. I've never seen such a thing!

With great anticipation,

Abaddon,

Disposable pets? How fantastic! Yes, emotions can be such a weakness and it seems like the Humans are driven by them. The king is making all of this far too easy for us. Jealousy is a great thing to exploit, spread it as much as possible.

What happens to the soul of the lifeless Human? We must claim every soul for our own purpose.

The Highest,

Patho

Chapter Nne

The years past, and as the population grew in Turayn, so did the hope of more Fallen Souls returning to the Kingdom. The King spent most of his time there, walking with anyone who allowed him. The King had met a certain man who seemed very familiar to him. The two spent a great deal of time together. The man's name was Gili. Gili dutifully made his sacrifices. He not only did it for himself, he made additional sacrifices for his children in the event they had done something they could not confess. Gili was a just and honorable man. He did everything with the highest level of integrity. Gili and the King seemed to have a connection that went far deeper than others who walked with the King.

In the early hours of the morning, while the dew was still blanketing the ground, the King made his way to Turayn where Gili was waiting. As they began their daily walk, Gili began to speak of things he had recently remembered. In recent days, these memories had become more and more vivid. He recalled a beautiful Kingdom with a magnificent castle. As he explained in detail the furnishings, the design and the gardens that surrounded the castle, the King realized it was his Kingdom Gili was describing.

The King desperately wanted to know who Gili was prior to Turayn. He was so familiar, like an old friend. But that information was impossible to obtain. The details of the selection process that allowed Fallen Souls to enter Turayn were highly protected. The requests received from the Fallen Souls were processed in a secret chamber deep within the castle. At no time was any one person allowed full access to a submitted request. The only information shared was the number of requests received on a particular day.

It was evening as the King and Queen walked arm in arm through the castle gardens.

"There's no way to tell," she said.

"I know, I know," the King replied.

"You'll just have to wait to see," she said.

""I never imagined it would be this difficult not knowing," said the King.

"It was your choice not to know," joked the Queen. "Perhaps the next time you can change the rules."

"Next time?" He said, "there will never be a 'next time'."

The following morning, the King left the castle earlier than usual. He was pleased to find Gili waiting for him. As they began their walk, Gili once again began to share his memories of the Kingdom. It was rare for a Human to remember any detail from their life before Turayn. If there was any recollection, it was usually about the Darkness and desperation they experienced after leaving the Kingdom. Gili was different. His memories went much further back. He began describing battles he had been fought; he was a leader of the warriors, second in command to the King.

A commander to the King? Gili described the battles in a way that the King recalled them as well. He knew this one. He had fought side by side with him. It was a staggering moment when the King realized who he was conversing with - the Human walking along side of him must be Waldemar.

Waldemar had once been the highest, bravest and most decorated warrior in his army. He had the King's complete trust and was part of every decision, even those of highest security. The moment the King learned that Waldemar had chosen to follow Patho was a moment like none other. His departure sent shock waves through the Kingdom. The King was well aware that his decision to leave helped Patho persuade multitudes more to follow him. Waldemar: warrior of all warriors, defender of the King, a confidante and friend.

Gili seemed to be unaware of time, lost so in his memories. It was a beautiful day in Turayn; a cool breeze tempered the heat from the sun. The King didn't want the day to end. They walked well into the afternoon.

"Tell me about the people in your vision," said the King.

"The King," Gili smiled. "The King was just. He was mighty. There was no one his equal," he said.

"Is this the King who led you in battle?" The King slowed the pace of their walking.

"Always, the King would never have expected someone to defend what he was not willing to defend himself," said Gili. The King smiled. This was a virtue He held highly. It was one He had taught each of his sons. A virtue they, too, had taken to heart.

"Did the King have sons?" the King asked.

"Yes, he did. I believe he had two." he stopped. Gili looked down and kicked a few stones from the path. "No," shaking his head, "there were more than that; there were two that left the Kingdom."

"Left - to go where?" inquired the King.

"I'm not sure. There must have been some type of separation." Remaining at a standstill, Gili gazed into the sky. The afternoon breeze had brought with it a thin layer of clouds coming from the east. Gili didn't really notice. He was looking far beyond the sky. "I know that two sons had parted ways with the King. One remained true to this decision, but the other," he stopped speaking. His expression moved from fond memories to pain. He closed his eyes and dropped his head. The King waited until Gili regained his composure. "The other regretted it the moment he stepped out through the gate."

"Regretted?" the King asked very gently.

Gili did not answer, he couldn't. Eventually, he forced the words out. "Yes, most regretted it," he whispered.

"We? Whom do you refer to?" asked the King. Gili took the first step and they began walking again. Their pace remained ever so slow as Gili was putting forth all his effort to remember. The King was in no hurry for their time together to come to an end.

"There were those who were deceived." Anger now filled Gili's voice. "He made promises of great things to come and distorted the truth about the King and his sons. It all happened so quickly. Many didn't understand the choice they were making until it was too late." Gili's pace quickened. This was the first time the King had witnessed a Fallen Soul remembering that day. He knew how emotionally charged such conversations were in the Kingdom. It had taken a great deal of time for He and the Princes to discuss those events without one of them igniting. Gili was feeling those same emotions. He was expressing the best he could in this human body. He continued. "There was great confusion. It was intolerable. We knew, once we left, there was no return."

They walked on. Gili was now in control of the pace. After a long silence, the King asked, "What happened next?"

"The next part," Gili paused, "is just darkness." Gili had stopped once again and was staring up into the heavens. "We were left wandering on our own. The Liar deserted us. All of his promises of battles were lies. There was nothing to conquer. He was the enemy." Gili stood silently, the King waited. "We would congregate as often as was safe, hoping—searching—for an answer. How would we get word back to the King? How would we plead for forgiveness?" Raising his voice and pounding his chest, he continued, "It was our choice. But we were wrong. We made the wrong decision."

The King was reliving that day himself. The pain, the ache he had experienced as he watched from the castle - unable to stop his subjects that blindly followed Patho. The emptiness that followed was at times almost inconceivable. The King recalled the day Jael spoke so passionately about the Fallen Souls. The day he knew they were ready to begin that journey, the day The Plan was born. "Was there any hope?" he eventually asked.

"No." Gili's voice cracked. He wrapped his arms around himself as if reminded of the loneliness he felt in the vastness. "Who would want to help us? With each meeting, we were putting ourselves in further danger. At some point, being in danger didn't even seem to matter; what could possibly be worse than to be separated from the King? We were so foolish." Gili took a long deep breath. The King and Gili walked on. "It was Quaine that kept us hoping. He was convinced the King would forgive us. He wrote endless requests. The last request was pleading for forgiveness: let us die out there in the Darkness, but let us die forgiven. The hope of ever entering the Kingdom had long since passed."

"The requests I have seen, have been received from Quaine," the King heard Jael's voice in his head. Those were once mere words. Quaine was leading a battle to find forgiveness, and he was leading it alone. He would have to fight it without help from his Father.

The King walked on. He reflected on The Plan. Those who would seek forgiveness: Waldemar was just that person. Waldemar had willingly made his sacrifice to the King. He had taught his sons and daughters the importance of seeking the Kings forgiveness through the practice of daily sacrifice. The King whispered gently, "I do forgive." The words rolled over the King's lips without a moment's hesitation. "Waldemar, I forgive, and I have longed to be able to bring you back into the Kingdom."

Waldemar stopped. He fell to the ground. In a moment, it was all clear. Every detail, every moment of separation, every memory of what once was, flooded his mind. The King reached down and helped him back to his feet.

"Jael read all of Quaine's requests. He was persistent, never allowing the hope for a plan of redemption to die." The King looked into Gili's eyes. They were full of wonder, fear, and love. "Jael kept the hope alive that one day there would be restoration. We created a plan that would allow full restoration for those who sought it."

Waldemar took a deep breath; the tightness in his chest had eased. He took another. The fogginess of his mind began to clear, his thoughts becoming brighter and more focused. With his next step, he realized that the pain of old age was gone. Then, Waldemar caught a glance of his hand. He stretched it out in front of him. He stretched out the other to compare. Where were the wrinkles? He rubbed his fingertips. They were soft; the calluses from years of hard labor were no more. He couldn't help but look down to his legs and feet. The rough gravel path was now smooth and calming. He ever so slowly looked toward the King. He could see Him. He couldn't move. For years, he and the King had walked together in Turayn, and he never realized the King was not visible. Here, standing in front of him, was his King, and he could see him. It took all his might to stay on his feet.

When he was finally able to move, he looked around at his surroundings. This was not the landscape of Turayn. The flowers that surrounded him were brilliant in color and aroma. He looked to his right and all he could see were gardens. He looked to his left. There, standing in the distance was the castle. How could this be? All hope had been lost that he would ever see this place again. He knelt down and felt the grass. Its' aroma was fragrant. He closed his eyes and took long deep breaths. The fragrances of the garden enveloped him. He was afraid to open his eyes, knowing that when he did, he would awaken. Biting his lips, he slowly opened them. It wasn't a dream. He was home.

The King, once again, helped Gili to his feet. The King's hand was warm and strong. If there was any doubt remaining, it left as soon as he took the King's hand. They walked slowly through the Gardens, the King leading the way. Waldemar was doing his best to keep up. But it was taking all his strength just to breathe. He wanted to stop and touch the flowers. He heard the birds singing. He had thought the birds in Turayn made beautiful sounds; he had forgotten the clarity and tone of those in the Kingdom. They passed a few gardeners working on a small flowerbed. Each acknowledged the King as he passed. Each took a double take as Waldemar passed.

The King slowly led him into the castle, stopping along the way for Waldemar to rest. Waldemar walked in disbelief of his surroundings. Beautiful seemed such an inadequate term to describe the Kingdom. No one had yet to transform from Turayn to the Kingdom with experiencing death on the other side. The King wasn't worried about the effects, but he wasn't going to rush Waldemar. "Give him time to acclimate," he kept repeating to himself.

Once in the corridor, Waldemar stopped walking. Realizing he was no longer in toe, the King turned around and went back to meet him. Waldemar leaned up against the wall. He stood tall with his head lifted up in the air, "I thought I had lost this." With both arms extended, Waldemar motioned to encompass all that surrounded him. "I hoped, but never believed, there would be a way back." He wiped a tear that escaped his efforts to stop them. "You are so just and merciful," Waldemar's voice cracked. "I'm sorry my Lord. It's hard for me to contain my emotions."

Pausing, he again looked around him. "It's impossible to express my gratitude. Before that dreadful day, this was all just part of life. This was where we lived and what we did. It was simply - life. I lost that life. Now this—all of this—is a gift. A gift I do not deserve." Waldemar knelt down on one knee. "In the past, it was not required to pledge our allegiance to you.

Who else would we serve? It's different now. I pledge to you my undying loyalty. With your forgiveness, I need only be the lowliest servant in your court. I deserve nothing more," said Waldemar.

"Waldemar, my dear friend." The King reached out, took his hand and helped him to his feet. "You have my forgiveness, and we'll have no more talk of it. Tonight, I want you to be my guest at our dinner table. I know that the boys will be thrilled to see you. The boys," the King chuckled. "I haven't called them that for years."

The King turn and continued through the corridors. Waldemar followed closely behind. With every step, memories of life in the Kingdom returned. He somehow managed to combine joy and humiliation into a way of walking. It was a stately stumble. As he made his way down the hall, he turned heads--some in recognition of who had returned, and others simply for his unique way of walking. He didn't know how to respond to the greetings from those in the castle. This couldn't be real. He must be in a deep sleep. He stopped pinching himself after his arm began to bruise.

As they approached the Dining Room, the King motioned to a passing attendant to stop. "Yes, Sire. What can I do for you?" the attendant asked as he bowed his head.

"There will be one more for dinner," the King replied.

"Yes, Sire. I'll inform the kitchen."

"And have someone inform the Queen that - he is here! She will know what I mean," instructed the King.

"Yes, Sire. Immediately!" The attendant bowed his head again but not before recognizing who was standing next to him. After the guest had passed, the attendant look up and then around him, hoping that he wasn't the only one to have witnessed this homecoming.

As the King and Waldemar approached the doors, the guard opened them and the King entered. Waldemar's heart was beating faster than he had ever experienced. He hesitated. How could he dine with the King? How could he face the Princes? This was happening too fast for his comprehension.

As Waldemar stood just outside the threshold not knowing if he should enter or make a run for it, the guard holding the door recognized him. Their eyes met. "Welcome home, Sir," he said. Waldemar lowered his head, unable to look him in the eye. "I wouldn't suggest running away, we did that already and it didn't turn out well."

"You?" Waldemar asked.

"Yes sir, me. The King is expecting you, you should go on in."

"I can't," Waldemar said.

"Yes, you can," the guard replied. "You can't live without him, you can follow him." Waldemar took a deep breath as the guard reached out and grabbed his arm. "It will be all right. They will welcome you home."

"This isn't happening," Waldemar whispered.

"Indeed it is, sir, and you need to experience it. Stand strong, He is waiting for you."

"Good evening, Father," Waldemar heard Magnor say from inside the room. He took a step in and stopped once again. "How was..." The room fell silent.

"Waldemar?" Magnor leapt to his feet. The others stayed motionless until the dawning of who had just entered filled them. The Dining Room echoed with greetings and laughter. The attendants could not help but take note. The guard wiped a tear.

"Yes, Waldemar! Welcome home!" The other four followed Magnor and each embraced him with the purest love and forgiveness ever offered.

"How did this happen? Father, how did you get to see him before the rest of us?" asked Jael. All five were huddled around Waldemar. Waldemar was bathed in hugs and his own tears.

"Do you remember me telling you about the human named Gili? Well, my sons, meet Gili!" The King said as he made his way to the end of the table. "I realized today who he was, and during our walk, he realized it as well," replied the King with great delight as he sat down.

"The King and I spent the day walking and reminiscing, and then suddenly I was home," added Waldemar. Jael put his arm around Waldemar and led him to a vacant seat; the very same chair Waldemar had occupied prior to leaving. Jael motioned for him to sit. Waldemar hesitated as if unable to move.

"Go ahead. Take your seat," Jael said as he patted Waldemar on the back.

Filling a goblet and offering it to their guest, Ferrul asked, "Father, how did you know?"

"Waldemar, you look good! It's wonderful to have you home," added Carasi, as he raised his goblet in toast.

"We need to talk about your adventures. I was there, you know," said Konnory excitedly. "Actually, I believe I would have been your great ..." Konnory leaned back in his chair, figuring the generations since he had been in Turayn.

"Excuse me?" Carasi said abruptly and with great concern. "You say you were walking and suddenly you were here?"

"Yes," The King replied. "Why wait any longer? He knew it. I knew it. I so longed for him to be home."

"But Father, you know the rules! You know the process!" said Ferrul.

"You insisted on it!" said Carasi.

"It was you who said, 'Without a process we'll run the danger of allowing Pathonians in without forgiveness.' Those were your words not ours, Father," Ferrul was wide eyed with concern.

"I know, I know. But its Waldemar," replied the King raising his goblet to his returned friend.

"Father," said Jael with a gentle laugh, "I understand. If I knew that Quaine was in Turayn, it would take all of you to hold me back. But there is too much at risk here: The Plan, forgiveness for those who seek it, and your Throne. We can't risk it, not for a moment." He knew just how much the King loved and missed Waldemar. There wasn't one of them that would refuse their Father this joy.

The King looked at Waldemar and said, "I told you they have grown into strong, wise warriors."

After taking a moment to look at each of the Princes, Waldemar said, "Yes, Sire, you did." Waldemar could not hold back the tears. He was home, in the presence of the King and the Princes, and he was forgiven.

Letters from the Pit

To his Highest, Patho,

We had explored every possibility as to what happens to the humans once life has left them. It appears they vanish in a puff of dust. There is no sign of them after they take their last breath.

As so, they seem to be disappearing while yet alive. Gilli, one who was disgusting in his seeing of the king and one who we were following closely, has vanished. Even his family seem unaware of his existence. We will continue to explore all possibilities.

Humbly,

Abaddon,

It is your job to know where these Human's are at every moment. Did you consider that perhaps they simply disintegrate after spending time seeking him? As if they need him. As if he has any authority in Turayn.

Your inadequacies are bothersome.

Highest,

Patho

To his brilliancy, Patho,

We have found a way to fully control some of the
Humans. The Law says that we can't do anything
without their permission, but doesn't really explain what we
can and can't do once we get the permission. It also doesn't
define what permission is required or how much of it. We
offer the more self-absorbed of them a bit of power to let us in
and then just take over their thoughts from within. Sometimes
they don't even realize they've agreed to it!

Humbly,

Abaddon,

That is finally good news indeed. Continue until we control every last one. The king will learn that there is nothing he can create that will not eventually become mine!

Highest,

Patho

To Patho and our fellow warlords in the Pit:

The Others have discovered that they can breed with the Humans. They are creating an entirely different race: strong, powerful, much larger Humans with a loyalty to the Pit from the moment they are born. We don't believe it is possible for them to seek forgiveness.

Your servant,

Abaddon,

A Pathonian half-breed? Extraordinary! I can only imagine
what they must look like. If they look anything like
their fathers, the Humans must be terrified of them. Turayn is
surely ours. Get them to multiply as quickly as possible. The
second and third generation should be even stronger and more
powerful. They may even become an army strong enough to
attack the Kingdom.

Highest,

Patho

Chapter Ten

The King hastily returned from his daily visit to Turayn. He rushed through the gardens and into the front corridor of the castle. As he headed toward the Dining Room, he bellowed, "Waldemar!"

Waldemar jumped. His heart began to race. It had been several weeks since he had returned, but he still could not get used to the King calling his name. He wondered if he lost something by returning so abruptly. Perhaps experiencing the human death would have prepared him more.

Since his return, the King would not hear of having him work any other place. It was ordered were given that Waldemar was to stay close. He was given small responsibilities in the castle, nothing too overwhelming. The King included him whenever possible in meetings and discussion. Waldemar would have been happy cleaning out the stables. He neither wanted or felt he deserved anything more.

"Waldemar!" He heard his name once again. This time it was stronger and more deliberate. Waldemar came around the corner as the King entered the Dining Room. It was quite obvious to anyone the King had passed that he was angered.

There had been a growing frustration following his recent visits, but today was different. Today, there was a great sense of urgency. "Waldemar, summon the Princes! I need them all!"

"Yes, Sire." Waldemar spun around on his heels and made his way to the Princes' chambers. All had retired for the night, except for Jael, who was doing his nightly reading. It brought such joy as he read aloud the names of each one. Some names he recognized.

Waldemar knocked on each door, informing each Prince of the summons. As quickly as they could, the Princes made their way to the King. Waldemar made a detour to the kitchen to inform them of the impromptu meeting that would undoubtedly last into the night. Bells rang and servants returned to their post in preparation for the night's event.

"Father, what's happened? What's wrong?" Konnory blurted out as he reached the Dining Room ahead of the others. Tucking his shirt into his trousers, Konnory was still putting himself back together. The King could hear the footsteps of the others making their way down the hall.

"He's done it again! He's found a loophole!!!" The King was pacing the length of the Dining Room.

The first servant entered with a tray of fruit, cheese, and bread. The wine steward and four additional attendants followed him. All-night meetings were not uncommon since The Plan had been initiated. There was no question what food or beverage would be required. There was as much commotion in the kitchen as in the Dining Room.

"Who? Who's done it again?" Konnory asked. The doors flew open as Carasi and Ferrul made their entrance.

"Who else but Patho?!" the King replied. "He and his - goons - have infested Turayn. And what's worse, his beasts have begun to breed with the Humans!" There was a collective groan of disgust by those in attendance. "They are mating with the human females. They are breeding! How could this happen? It has to stop. I'm ending it! It's over!"

"Father, Father, slow down," Konnory said forcefully. "We knew he would get into Turayn; we designed it that way."

Jael and Magnor were the last to enter. Waldemar stuck his head in the door, assuring the King was being served. As an attendant made his exit, Waldemar pulled him aside. "Remind the kitchen to begin the King's Draught," Waldemar instructed.

During the early days, when the outline was being drawn up for The Plan, the King had made His way to the kitchen searching for a hot beverage. It was either the late night or the long day that made the typical beverages seem bland. Perhaps it was the fact that the King was surrounded by such an enormous level of creativity, it inspired Him to create a new beverage, which he named King's Draught. There was only one person in the kitchen that knew its ingredients. She just happened to be passing through that night of the King's inspiration and was sucked into the experiment. Since then, at every night meeting, this single attendant made her way to the kitchen to prepare a large caldron of King's Draught.

"But breeding?!" Magnor shouted out. "I'm not sure we thought they would breed! Who would find the Others breed-able? Just the thought makes me shudder."

Konnory looked at Magnor. Both cringed. Returning his attention to the King, "You also gave authority to Jael to end The Plan, and I don't believe he has returned it to you." Konnory looked at Jael for reassurance.

"Wait! Wait! Breeding!?" Magnor's expression was a combination of confusion and disgust. "This doesn't make sense. The Others aren't human! How is that even possible?"

Ferrul had taken his seat and took a deep breath, "All I can figure is that one or several of the Humans allowed Patho's cohorts to have control of them." As he finished talking, he began looking around. Spotting a stack of tablets, Ferrul jumped out of his chair, grabbed a tablet, a handful of writing utensils, and sat back down.

"How does that work?" Jael questioned. Jael looked at Magnor. They shared looks of disgust. "No spirit has any authority in Turayn. It's a law."

"Correct, Jael," Ferrul continued, "No spirit has authority or can take control of a human unless requested. That includes them as well as us. If they have done this forcefully, then they have broken the Laws and we have the power to end it, or at least remove the guilty parties." Ferrul opened the tablet and began vigorously sketching. He quickly turned the page and continued.

"Yes, we have to put a stop to this!" Magnor said. He was too disturbed to sit down. He walked to the serving table and filled a plate. It was much more than he would normally take, but he wasn't thinking about food. All he could envision were the horrifying faces of the Others that he had seen. *Who could possibly breed with that,* he thought.

Carasi joined the discussion. "Patho and his warlords are offering to coexist with the humans if they would allow them access to their bodies. But we know very well, Patho does not co-anything with anyone. Once they are allowed in, they take total control." Carasi grabbed a handful of empty tablets and took the seat next to Ferrul. He began making notes.

"But that doesn't answer the breeding issue," said Magnor.

"Patho has joined forces with many of those who left the Kingdom long ago," said Carasi, as he continued writing. "These are the ones who are breeding. They have found a way to impregnate the human female."

"It may actually be possible that the Others have found a way to take human form," Ferrul offered.

"If they can take human form..." Magnor said.

"The Watchers have done it on a few occasions," Ferrul said.

"But that would have been to do good, right?" Magnor asked.

"Of course. But if Watchers can take human form, it's reasonable to think Others can as well," Carasi said.

"I want it over! Let's wipe them all out and start over!" shouted the King, who continued pacing the full length of the Dining Room.

"I'm sorry, Father, but that's not an option," said Ferrul. "If we wipe them all out, we can't start over. Ferrul continued drawing. "Is there not someone who would make The Plan worth saving, or is it truly time to bring it to an end?" Ferrul asked.

The King never looked up. He paced with hands locked behind his back, "No! There is not!" he answered.

Ferrul stopped and looked directly at the King, "There isn't one human that you have a relationship with? If that's the case, why do you spend so much time there? We have to come up with a solution, but we can't just go over there and act on our own accord. We need someone to work with, someone who can give arms and legs to our mission. So back to my question, is there anyone there that you think would be able to assist us?"

The King stopped to consider. "Latzof. Latzof is a good one," said the King, as he began walking again.

"A good one? That's all you can come up with? A good one?" responded Carasi.

"No, no, no. Latzof is good! He's of the highest integrity; he's very honorable in all that he does," the King said.

Konnory walked over to where Ferrul and Carasi were sitting and looked over their shoulders. With a loud burst of laughter, Konnory gave both brothers pats on their shoulders. Carasi and Ferrul looked up at Konnory. They smiled and returned to their work.

Carasi asked, "Is Latzof someone who will follow your directions? Will he do it without question? Is he capable of following instructions with little assistance?"

"Yes, I am sure he would be able and willing to do so." The King was finally standing behind his chair. He pulled it out and settled in.

"Will wiping them out prevent it from ever happening again?" Jael questioned. He, too, was curious as to what his brothers were up to. He had taken a seat directly across from them. Stretching to see what the tablets contained, he closed his eyes, put his head back, and smiled.

"Part of it," Ferrul assured. "We cannot stop the Humans from opening themselves up to Patho and his warlords. That will be a battle we fight until the end. But we will be able to stop those who are breeding."

"Let's burn the whole thing!" said the King.

"That's an option, but how do we protect Latzof?" said Carasi.

"Let's freeze it all and start all over," said the King.

"Not an option. Latzof could never survive the thaw. By the way, how old is he?" inquired Ferrul.

"He is fairly old but very strong. He is a very able sort," responded the King. "What does that have to do with freezing and thawing?"

"Nothing," Carasi answered. He leaned into Ferrul and he whispered, "but given his age he'll just appear insane." Both Jael and Konnory heard his comment and burst into laughter simultaneously. Carasi gave both a stern look and the laughter stopped. Carasi smirked. "Does he have sons?"

"Yes, he has five," answered the King. He reached for the goblet.

"That could be one of his reasons for insanity," Carasi said, half under his breath. Everyone but Magnor began to chuckle; however hushed they tried to be, it didn't matter. The more they held it in, the funnier it all became. The attendants couldn't help but notice the contrast between the King's frustration and Jael and Konnory's laughter. And one could only imagine what was playing in Magnor's mind. It took every ounce of control for the attendants and servants that were in the room to not be sucked into the laughter.

"Are Latzof's sons trustworthy?"

"I believe they are. Why do you ask?" the King asked insistently.

"We are going to need to repopulate," Carasi said. "Starting over now takes us back to the beginning. Latzof may not be able to reproduce as quickly as we need at his age. His sons would allow us to repopulate much faster." Carasi continued writing.

"Wait! Wait!" Magnor had a rare expression of total confusion. "We can't wipe them out, what will happen to the Fallen Souls?"

The room came to a dead stop. Both Carasi and Ferrul looked up from their work. They looked at each other and then towards their brother. "Magnor, so you do care about the Fallen Souls?" they said in unison. Magnor huffed and turned away.

"He does have a heart," echoed from the far end of the room.

"It's not an issue," Ferrul answered. "Those who have sought forgiveness will find themselves back in the Kingdom. Those who have not will return to the Darkness." Carasi and Ferrul continued working.

"I've searched Turayn," said the King, "and I am unable to find even ten who are seeking forgiveness. If we don't do something, this will all come to an end very quickly." Waldemar reentered the room. In his hands was the caldron. The King's eyes lit up. Waldemar poured a cup of King's Draught and handed it to the King. With great delight, the King took the first sip. "Perfect!" he said, "Just as I remember. I wish I could get the Queen to learn to make this."

"She's much too wise for that," Magnor said. "She prefers allowing you to have this one secret!"

After a few more delightful sips, the King's mood had calmed. He stood and began to walk to the windows. "I have it! Let's just wash everything away! We'll send rain like Turayn has never seen. I could open the depths of the seas and cause a great torrent: water from above and below coming together to wash Turayn clean!" the King was greatly excited about the prospect.

Jael glanced across the table. "I believe that could work!" he said with an assuring nod.

"We'll need a way to rescue Latzof, of course," added the King. Konnory's body began to shake. Ferrul could hold back no longer, and he let out a stifled laugh. Carasi just shook his head.

"What do you find so humorous?" demanded the King.

"Nothing, Father, go on," Jael said speaking for Konnory. "How do you think we should rescue Latzof?"

"We can give him a boat," said the King.

"We can give him a boat?" questioned Magnor, with just a hint of sarcasm in his tone. "Why don't we just bring Latzof and his family here for the time being and then put him back when it's all over." Konnory was now bent over in his chair, clutching his stomach and doing everything within his power to not lose control over the laughter boiling up inside of him.

"That is an excellent idea!" the King said wide-eyed.

"No Father," Ferrul responded, "but I do think the boat idea will work. We can't give it to him; it would cause too much commotion. He'll have to build it himself."

"Yes, that works very well!" Carasi replied.

"Let's not stop there," said Magnor. "If we can salvage Latzof, let's attempt to salvage the creatures as well. Some of my best handiwork is there." Magnor had finally made his way over to where Ferrul and Carasi were working. He continued, "We'll need a craft that can house the Humans and two of each of the creatures..." Magnor stopped. He studied Carasi and Ferrul's drawings. Pointing down he asked, "That's why it has so many levels, isn't it?" Carasi smiled. Magnor shook his head, "I'll never understand how your minds work," he said and walked away.

Konnory fell off his chair in laughter. Carasi looked over at him lying on the floor; arms wrapped around his middle, laughing uncontrollably. Without changing his expression, Carasi shook his head again. This, of course, fueled Jael's laughter; he so loved Konnory's sense of humor. He knew that only Carasi could witness such a happening and not be affected by it.

Magnor ignored the entire episode. Two attendants made their way to Konnory's side, but by this time his laughter was contagious. As the two helped him back to his seat, the three were now a chorus of laughter. The King sat at the end of the table wide-eyed as if he was watching a play, but still unsure why it was being played out before him.

With his tablet in hand, Ferrul stood and made his way to the King's side. Showing him the drawing, the King nodded in great delight.

"Father, you'll need to deliver the instructions to Latzof. If Patho gets wind of any discussion, he'll have his..," Carasi paused and smiled, "Goons, as you call them, swarming in an instant. Latzof needs to receive your instructions and move quickly...quickly, but quietly. This has to stay out of Patho's detection."

"If there is any resistance," Ferrul warned, "we need to know immediately in order to come up with a new solution. If Patho suspects anything, it puts everything in danger."

"I'll take Waldemar with me!" the King said with great enthusiasm. Shock and terror filled Waldemar at the thought.

"NO!" All five sons responded at once.

"You can't risk it! If 'his ugliness' got wind of that..." Magnor rolled his head back.

The Princes worked all night and so did the servants. As the morning light made its way through the windows, they finalized the boat's design. Ferrul gathered all the instructions and handed them to Father.

"One last thing," Carasi said. "Latzof will have to appear as if he has gone mad. In doing so, Patho won't give him a second thought."

"That won't be difficult," said the King. "We're asking him to build a boat in the middle of a field that is large enough to house an army. Patho's not the only one who will see him as crazy!" With a nod of their heads, the King took hold of the instructions and made his way to his daily walk with Latzof.

As always, Latzof awaited the King. As they walked, the King began to unveil what was ahead and the important role he would play in all of it. Without a moment's hesitation, Latzof accepted the instructions. As the King went over every detail, Latzof's only questions were for clarification, he took notes as to not forget.

The King was delighted in Latzof's willingness. There was no doubt he would follow the instructions completely. Latzof began his work immediately. This was a task that would take almost a lifetime to complete. He needed to be as unsuspecting as possible so not to draw attention.

The King checked on him regularly. He was pleased to see Latzof's sons working alongside him. This was a task Latzof would not have been able to complete on his own. It reminded the King of the days spent creating The Plan. As Latzof got closer to completing the boat, plans were laid for the final steps.

The day had come, the boat was complete and all supplies had been stored away. The King instructed Latzof and his family to board the craft. The King then called by name two of each of the animals that roamed Turayn. He made sure he called animals from different regions to keep Abaddon off base. A stampede of creatures would undoubtably draw someone's attention. It was a sight to behold; creatures from all across Turayn hearing and responding to the voice of their Creator. The creatures willingly found their way to the boat, as if they had found their way home.

The Pit eventually heard of Latzof's boat. Patho was not a stranger to Turayn; he had visited many times. He felt, however, that it was better for him to spend most of his time in the Pit. It gave him a sense of authority, but this was something he had to see. There had been a report of a crazy old man building a boat in the middle of a field. The only water was a small river about hundred yards away. Patho was escorted to the site. As he drew closer, he saw the door close. Patho was outraged. As he began to send out summons to his warlords, the first raindrops began to fall.

"What is this!" Patho shouted. "Water falling from the sky? I hate water!! Get me out of here!" Patho made his way to the end of Turayn. His warlords quickly followed.

As designed, the rain fell in great amounts. The King made the waters held deep below the surface break free of their boundaries and consume Turayn. With the waters from above and floods from below, Turayn was soon engulfed and the Others' offspring were trapped. There was no escape.

It took several years for the waters to completely subside. Latzof and his sons had done as they had been asked without question. In doing so, they assisted the King in clearing Turayn of those that sought to destroy it. Turayn had been given a fresh start. The Humans were once again just that—Humans. There was little chance that any Pathonian-half-breed would corrupt the human race again.

As the years passed, Turayn's landscape recovered from the flood. The lush vegetation filled the hillsides as the waters returned to their boundaries. Turayn was once again operating as intended.

Letters from the Pit

To all Warlords, Pathonians and Others who serve the Pit,

Victory is mine! The king has destroyed all of the life that he created on that foolish world of his. We may have lost the half-breeds, but provoking the king to such an extent and ruining his little project is well worth it. I have beaten him yet again!

Your Highest,

Patho

Chapter Eleven

The King and his sons had just settled in for dinner when Waldemar burst into the room. "He's here, he's here!" shouted Waldemar.

"Who's here?" asked Konnory.

"Tayten!" said Waldemar. Silence fell across the room.

"Tayten?" Konnory repeated, as he sat back in his chair. The others sat speechless.

Waldemar looked around the room. He knew that this news would bring a level of excitement, but he greatly underestimated the possibility and enormity of the initial shock. "Yes, he has just arrived," replied Waldemar.

The King sat upright. He leaned forward and rested his arms on the table. Tayten was a trusted friend, a scholar. He was the Princes' tutor, mentor, and confidante. Tayten had tutored each Prince as a child. As they matured, Tayten worked with each to develop their character. He spent his life committed to the growth and development of each one.

Tayten had an overpowering stature. His height equaled that of Magnor and Jael's. As children, Tayten towered over the Princes like a friendly giant. He had a gentle but authoritative manner. There wasn't a topic he couldn't discuss, not a theory he was afraid to question. He had not only invested his time in the Princes, he had also invested himself.

When word had arrived that Tayten had left, it was a loss the Princes had never known. In some ways, they felt deserted and abandoned. Konnory had been the most affected. He did his best to try and understand, to make sense of Tayten's decision, but to no avail. Konnory had carried the pain deeply.

The room was silent for an awkwardly long period of time. Then, all at once, chairs, serving pieces, goblets, and papers were sent flying in all directions, as the five fought for the lead position. The servants and attendants in the room backed up to the walls in order to get out of the way. Konnory won the competition and darted out the door first. It made the King smile. It had been a long time since such joy had been felt in the castle. As he pushed his chair back, Waldemar made his way over.

"Tayten, hmmm?" said the King.

"Yes, Sire. He is home," replied Waldemar.

"I had hoped. Konnory has carried this pain the deepest," said the King.

Waldemar motioned for any remaining attendants to leave. When the room was finally empty, he pulled out the chair next to the King and seated himself. "Sire, I have a question?" asked Waldemar.

The King was somewhat surprised at Waldemar's directness. At the same time, He was relieved. He had waited to see Waldemar's confidence return. "Yes, what is it?" he asked.

"Sire, that day—that horrific day—those of us," Waldemar put his head down. He was always so humbled by these memories. "Those of us that left, it was our choice. You allowed us Free Will; it was something we had taken for granted until that day. I have watched as the redeemed have reentered the Kingdom. I watch as Jael reads through the names each night, at times reading through his tears. I experienced it the day you brought me back. You and the Princes, for that matter everyone in the Kingdom, welcomed us back openly. There was no judgment. There was no questioning. It felt as if I had simply been lost and found my way home, although it wasn't that at all. Why is that? How is that possible?"

"Waldemar, my friend," The King shook his head. "When we began to talk of The Plan, we first defined how forgiveness would be offered. It was decided it would be given freely to any Fallen Soul who sought after it. It's as simple as that; it is given freely."

"Freely? I don't understand. All of this comes with a great price..." said Waldemar.

The King reached out and took Waldemar's forearm. "Forgiveness is given freely. It is the act of forgiveness that costs everything. In order for one to give forgiveness, one must relinquish the right to ask for justification. Yes, there is great cost. A great cost indeed."

"But are there not consequences?" questioned Waldemar.

"Certainly, there are. You know from your own experience about such consequences. You, who once stood by my side ready for battle, now stands by my side to ensure that I am ready for battle. Consequences fall on the one forgiven. We live under this Law of Consequence. When you plant a seed, a tree begins to grow. Every action has a consequence."

"And what of the sacrifices?" asked Waldemar.

"Oh yes, the sacrifice," the King replied, as a soft and gentle smile replaced the serious expression from the previous topic. "A sacrifice is not a means of offering forgiveness; it's a means of remembering that forgiveness is always available. You could have offered a tadpole every day, but if it was the best tadpole you caught and you offered that tadpole with a sincere heart, I would have accepted it. You needed to make the sacrifice to remind yourself that forgiveness was available, and that forgiveness was required." The King was quiet for a few moments. Waldemar was deep in thought.

"Enough," said the King. "Tell me, who was Tayten? You must have seen his file. Please tell me he held a great position." Waldemar smiled and shook his head. He rose to his feet.

The King waited for Waldemar's response, which appeared to be delayed. "Please don't tell me he was a farmhand that tended to the cattle or cleaned out the stalls," said the King.

Waldemar tilted his head just slightly. "Well, he wasn't until you asked him to!"

"I asked him to. What are you talking about? I never asked anyone-" the King paused, lowering his eyebrows. "Don't tell me…"

Waldemar hesitated, partly to create more anticipation, and partly because he was enjoying the irony. He turned and began to walk to the door.

The King stood and followed after him. Chuckling to himself, he demanded, "Don't keep me waiting, man!"

Waldemar opened the door and looked back, "He was Latzof; the crazy old man who built a boat," he said.

The King let out a howl that echoed through the castle. As they entered the courtyard, the King's laughter had grown to a bellow that was heard throughout the gardens.

Letters from the Pit

To Patho our true conqueror,

Turayn is dry again. Enough Humans and creatures survived to begin repopulating. Apparently the lunatic with the boat wasn't as crazy as we had hoped. We have resumed all of our regular tactics with the exception of the half-breeds, of course.

Your servant,

Abaddon

To Abaddon,

While this may seem like a setback, we have controlled the Humans on Turayn from the start, and we will continue to do so now.

I have decided on the first act of retribution against the king for destroying all the work we had done so far; begin introducing the idea that there are many other things that the Humans should worship in place of the king. I will leave the choices up to you, but I would suggest using animals, possessions, even other gods; whatever you can think of to drive a wedge between the Humans and the king.

Highest,

Patho

To Patho our only conqueror,

We have been able to convince many of the Humans that there are other, more worthy objects of their worship than the king. Quite a few of them have even begun offering their sacrifices to these other gods instead. There have been reports that some groups are now sacrificing other Humans to their gods. I did not realize that this would also drive such a large wedge between the Humans based on what they worshipped.

Your servant,

Abaddon

To Abaddon,

I must admit, even I did not think that those fools would begin sacrificing each other! I am sure the king will be most thrilled with that little turn of events. Well done. However, I must warn you, your addresses are becoming undesirably repetitive.

Highest,

Patho

Chapter Twelve

J ael was halfway down the stairs when he realized Konnory was close behind. "Going somewhere?" he asked.

"Just thought I would tag along this evening," Konnory said.

"Really?" Jael asked. "All right, I guess?"

The two brothers made their way through the corridors of the castle, descended another flight of stairs, where they found themselves at the entrance to a long hallway. At the end were large guarded doors. The guards saluted the brothers as they entered.

"You've been here before?" Jael asked.

"Yes, but it's been awhile," Konnory said.

As the doors closed behind them, the two stood observing the activity of the room. Jael was warmly greeted, "Good evening Sir, it's good to see you again today."

"Thank you," he replied.

"And you, Sir," the attendant said addressing Konnory, "Welcome. Will you be joining Jael this evening?"

Jael looked at Konnory in anticipation of his answer. He was still unsure of the reasoning behind this unexpected accompaniment.

"No, but I would like to spend time observing – it's quite a busy place, isn't it?" Konnory said.

"That it is Sir," the attendant said with a smile and nod. "Spend all the time you need and please don't hesitate to ask questions. I know you will find everyone eager to assist."

"I'll be right over here," Jael said pointing to the corner of the room. Konnory glanced over and saw a table and chair that had been prepared for him. On the table lay a large book. Konnory watched as Jael walked over to the table and sat down. He adjusted his chair and sat quietly with his hands clasped resting on the book. After a few moments, Jael opened the book. Konnory walked closer. It was a large ledger, filling almost the entire width of the table. The pages were filled with names, line after line of names. As soon as Jael's eyes hit the page, Konnory could see that nothing else mattered. Jael read each name aloud; slowly, intentionally, pausing after each. These were the names of those who had returned to the Kingdom.

Konnory smiled. He knew Jael spent much time here. He had kidded his brother about his nightly readings, but watching Jael made him understand. He could not help but see the love on Jael's face as he read the names of the redeemed. The excitement when he read a name he knew, and the passion when he read groups of names that were undoubtedly entire families.

Konnory walked around the room, the attendant followed. He pointed to another set of doors. They were propped open leading to a long hallway that was lined with more doors. "Where does that lead?" he asked.

"That is storage," the attendant replied. "This is where all the files are stored for those who have returned to the Kingdom."

"Those rooms are all filled with files?" he asked.

"No, Sir, however we expect that some day they will be," the attendant said.

"This would be a great place to work," Konnory said.

"Yes, this is the end of the journey. This is proof that The Plan is working."

The wall behind Konnory was lined with shelves. "What are these?" he asked as he pointed to files that almost filled the bottom row. "Are they waiting to be filed?"

The attendant smiled. "These are the files of those who have lived an - how should I put this – an unusual life in Turayn."

"Unusual?" Konnory said. "Are there any lives that aren't usual?"

The attendant laughed, "You would know better than anyone," he said. "Each life in Turayn is unusual. Those rooms down the hall are being filled with files of all those who lived," he paused. "Lived the usual, unusual lives. But there are some whose lives in Turayn are measured differently."

"Based on what they accomplished?" Konnory asked.

"No Sir," the attendant was quick to reply. "It is based on," he paused, "how they lived." Konnory contemplated these words. The attendant continued, "Some of these may have accomplished great things, others lived simple lives. What they have in common is how they lived, their connection with the King and their passion for their fellow Humans. As each file is read, there are those that stand out, we have separated their files. Some of these stories have already become important in Turayn."

Konnory knelt down and began to read the names. Seeing Waldemar's file made him smile. Latzof's file was present. "Do I have a file?" he asked.

"Yes you do, but you will not find it here. Your Father has that one," the attendant said grinning from ear to ear. Konnory nodded.

"I'm not familiar with these other names," Konnory said.

"Perhaps you would like to read through some," the attendant offered. "Take a few with you, I have to say, it is delightful reading."

Konnory scanned the files once again. There were several that seemed to jump out at him. After choosing a small group of them, he stood and observed the activity in the room again.

"I would suggest you go through those doors. I'll be happy to hold these for you, and you can pick them up before you leave," the attendant offered as he took the files from Konnory.

"How long will he be here?" Konnory asked pointing to Jael.

"We are never sure," the attendant said.

Konnory walked toward the doors and found himself at the top of a stairwell. As he began to descend, he couldn't help but notice the increase of noise and activity. When the entire room was in his sight, he stood and watched. In the center of the room was a large chair, almost the size of Father's throne. Around the parameter of the room were small tabletops surrounded by three or four chairs. Konnory noticed that there was a stack of files on each table. He also noticed that there was only one attendant seated at each, some appeared to be talking to themselves. No one noticed his entrance as they were focused on the work in front of them.

Konnory walked over to the chair in the center of the room. He reached down and felt the carvings on the arm. Something brushed by his side. He turned to look, but there was no one there. At the far end of the room were yet another set of guarded doors. Konnory made his way toward them. As he approached, the guards saluted. Konnory nodded and reached for the handle.

"I'm sorry, Sir, but you are not allowed in there," the guard instructed.

Konnory stepped back. At that moment, the door opened and a small group of workers made their exit. Each was surprised to see their visitor and each greeted him. When the last one had made his exit, the guards closed the door and stood once again at attention.

"Oh I see," Konnory said. "You can come out, but you can't go in - interesting." The guards smiled but did not respond.

"May I help you, Sir?" Konnory turned and found a rather short, at least he was short in Konnory's acquaintances, standing next to him. "Is there anything particular you are looking for?"

"It was recommended that I come down to see the operations here," Konnory said.

"It's wonderful to have you. My name is Balbas. We expect to see the King, but it's a rarity when one of his sons finds their way here," he said, with great delight.

"The King?" Konnory asked.

"Yes, that is his throne chair. When he is not in Turayn, he spends much of his time here." Konnory felt something brush against his arm and turned to look. "Oh, don't mind them; it gets so crowded down here sometimes," Balbas said.

Konnory looked around the room. This was one of the largest rooms in the castle. There could have been a hundred tables circling the perimeter but the center of the room was open. "What do you mean, it gets so crowded?" Again, something brushed his other arm, and he quickly turned to look.

"Is this your first time here?" Balbas asked. Konnory nodded. "Give it a moment." The attendant stood watching Konnory who began to feel a bit self-conscious.

Trying to take the attention off of himself, he pointed to the guarded doors, "Where does that lead?"

"This is your first time here," he said. "That houses the selection process."

"Selection?"

"Yes, that is where the Fallen Souls' requests are processed," said Balbas.

"I saw workers coming out," said Konnory.

"It is the exit, we only ever see them coming out."

"Where's the entrance?" asked Konnory.

"One only knows," said Balbas. "Hold on, I need to catch them." The attendant waved his hand in the air and shouted, "Wait! Wait!" Turning back to Konnory he said, "I'll be right back, just have to give some last minute instructions." With that, Balbas darted toward the stairs.

Konnory watched as he stopped and began talking. Balbas was quite dramatic when he spoke. It seemed overly dramatic since Konnory did not see to whom he was speaking. There wasn't anyone standing in front of or next to Balbas. Konnory scanned the room, and when his eyes returned to the conversation, nothing had changed. Balbas stood speaking, but no one was listening.

"He's been down here too long," Konnory said to himself. He continued watching. Balbas seemed to be having a two way conversation. In fact, he kept turning his head as if he were talking to more than just one person. Once again, something brushed Konnory's arm. As he turned, he caught a glimpse. He stood staring. He blinked as a vague image passed by. He blinked again, his vision became clearer and clearer. Within a few moments, they became visible to him. Konnory scanned the room, it was filled with - Watchers. They surrounded the tables; they were in groups throughout the room. The only place they weren't was a small circle around the throne chair.

Konnory was very familiar with the Watchers; they had been a part of his world as a Human. In Turayn, however, they chose when and who could see them. When they returned to the Kingdom, their presence was always felt, but it took a patient eye to observe.

Konnory looked over to Balbas. He was surrounded by about ten Watchers. Konnory watched in amazement. They were magnificent. After the attendant had finished, he made his way back to Konnory.

"So sorry about that, we have a bit of a situation that needs their immediate attention. Tell me, what questions do you have?"

"What goes on here?" Konnory asked.

"Ah, yes, let's start at the beginning." He took Konnory's arm and began to walk around the room. "Every human is assigned at least one Watcher from the time they enter Turayn. It only takes a few days for the Watcher to begin to foresee the Human's personality, gifts, and talents. It's all coincidental, by the way. There is no formula that dictates who gets what personality. None of them are born with an instruction sheet. Wouldn't that be lovely? But everyone has a unique personality and an abundance of gifts and talents that have to be discovered. The Watchers can sense, within a few short days, what those are. That information is sent here, where we begin to determine the protection that is needed."

"Protection?" Konnory needed clarification.

"We know what Patho's big plan of attack is," the attendant said waving his hands in the air. "He has only one, you know. You would think by now he would have developed something new." Balbas shook his head in disgust. Konnory laughed. "Patho's does everything in his power to attack these innocent little Humans with fear. Fear – that's it. He's got nothing else. Well, some say he uses deception. It's true. I'll give him that.

But I'm not totally convinced that deception isn't an outcome of fear. The jury is still out on that one."

"The Watchers report back here and a strategy is created. Some may require additional Watchers. It's the creative ones that seem to need more guidance. Patho targets the creative and the intelligent. He keeps the creative ones so self-conscious that they don't use their gifts and, he distracts the intelligent ones, keeping them focused on unimportant matters. They rarely discover just how much good they could do, it's such a shame." He lowered his head. His name was called from across the room. Balbas turned and motioned that it would be a moment and then pointed at Konnory. Turning his attention back, he continued, "Meetings are held regularly to keep all up to date. Priority is to direct them back to the King and to seek forgiveness. Helping them to use their gifts and talents to do good is second."

Balbas paused for the briefest second, "They go hand-in-hand you know. Doing good always brings them back to the King." Balbas spun around to face the center of the room.

"You have undoubtedly seen the King's chair?" he continued. "We refer to it as the 'throne away from throne' because, of course, the real throne is in the real Throne Room." Balbas made an imaginary outline of a box with his fingers. "But you know that, you've been there." Konnory began to chuckle. "Oh, you'll have to excuse me, I'm so used to having ten conversations going on around me - I can ramble at times." Konnory assumed this was the end of the explanation, but it wasn't.

"Where was I? Oh, yes, *the throne away from throne.* The King spends much of his time down here, that is, when he isn't in Turayn. He is always a part of the conversation. The Watchers will alert him if they feel there may be someone who needs his attention. No doubt you've seen the files upstairs? The King was personally involved with several of them. They come up with crazy plans sometimes. If the Humans had any idea the amount of time put into each of them... There is an entire universe working non-stop to do everything possible for them to find their way home.

"As I recall from the file, you had well over fifty Watchers assigned to you? There was also a regiment of warriors who stayed close at all times. The only real protection you needed, I believe, was from Magnor." Balbas began to laugh. "He and those stupid trees. He will get the timing right one of these times."

Konnory waited for Balbas to continue. *Perhaps, he has finally run out of air,* he thought. "How long have you worked here?" Konnory asked after a moment of silence.

"Ever since my time on Turayn came to an end; I still don't know exactly where that arrow came from," he responded. "Don't want to go anywhere else. In there," he pointed to the guarded doors, "they are reading requests and assigning Fallen Souls to human vessels. Upstairs is where it ends. Here is where it lives! We are fighting battles every minute of every day for the Fallen Souls. We are at war. I would not be any place else.

Konnory reached out and shook Balbas's hand. "With you here, how could we fail? Welcome home."

"Thank you, Sir," Balbas bowed his head. "It is my honor and privilege. To be able to work with the King again is beyond any hope I had. If you will excuse me, Sir, I have several more meetings to attend before this day comes to an end for me."

"Don't let me keep you," Konnory said. Balbas spun around and headed toward a table on the far end of the room, he was surrounded by Watchers.

Konnory walked around the room, listening to the discussions. Each was different. Each was specific. But each was filled with hope. He walked past the 'throne away from the throne' and reached down to feel the armrest. He envisioned Father sitting there surrounded by Watchers discussing one of the Human's plight. He wondered what those conversations were like when he was living in Turayn.

Heading back up the stairs, Konnory was eager to pick up the files he had chosen earlier and begin reading. When he got to the top of the stairs, he saw that Jael's chair was empty and had already been reset for his next visit.

"Here are the files," the upstairs attendant said, as he handed them to Konnory. "I'm sure you will enjoy your reading."

"Thank you," Konnory said. "You can be sure I'll return."

"Would you like for us to set up a table for you as we do for Jael?"

"That won't be necessary. I'll do my reading in the gardens." Konnory walked to the door and grabbed the handle. He turned around to once again watch the movement of the room. "All this is for them." As he walked through the doors, he could feel his eyes begin to well up.

Konnory reached the top of the stairs and realized daylight was illuminating the hallway. *Was I really down there all night?* he thought. To his right was the Dining Room, to his left the gardens. Waldemar appeared at the end of the hallway.

"Good morning, Sir, will you be joining us?" Waldemar called out.

"That is just what I was standing here deciding," Konnory answered.

Waldemar saw the files in Konnory's hand. He walked past the Dining Room and approached Konnory. "You've been down there, I see," he said.

"Yes. It looks as though I spent the night." Konnory looked down at the files. "I'm rather eager to get to these. Would it be too much of an inconvenience to have someone bring my breakfast out there?" Konnory pointed toward the gardens.

"Not at all, I'll bring it myself," Waldemar offered. "You don't have my file in there, do you?"

"No. But I did see it. I think I know all I need to know about your return." The two laughed. "I'll be outside. I'm really not that hungry. Whenever you have a moment, I would appreciate it."

"Enjoy your reading," Waldemar said, as Konnory turned and walked down the corridor.

Chapter Thirteen

Konnory walked out into the gardens. The warmth of the light and fresh morning breeze enveloped him. The groundskeepers were engrossed in several projects. A new walkway was being laid and new flowerbeds were being planted. Konnory decided to settle in next to the stream where the water babbled over the rocks. He loved it's comforting sound. It would make a great backdrop for his day of reading.

Making himself comfortable, he laid the files out. Randomly choosing his first file, he leaned back and opened it with great excitement.

Nadav was written at the top of the page. He began reading:

For generations, Nadav's family had sought forgiveness. The King walked with his father and grandfather. The youngest of twelve boys, Nadav found great favor in his father's house. This favor created great jealousy in his brothers. Nadav's father didn't hide his favoritism for Nadav, which brought even deeper resentment and hatred from the brothers.

As a boy, the King visited Nadav in his dreams; many times showing him glimpses of his future. In one of these dreams, the King showed him of a time when his brothers would bow down to him; he would have authority over them. This revelation excited the young lad but did not find favor with his brothers.

In an attempt to rid themselves of the constant reminder of the great love their father had for Nadav, they planned to throw him into a large pit hoping he would die. The stage was set as the brothers asked Nadav to join them on a day's journey. With great excitement, Nadav accepted.

A distance from home, the convoy reached the location of the pit. All the anger, resentment, and jealousy that had built up in them erupted. They took the young lad and taunted and teased him, ripped his coat from him and threw him into the depths of the pit. He lay there bruised and bleeding as he listened to their laughter, accusation, and then, the laughter fade in the distance.

Cold and alone, Nadav called out to the King. To his surprise, the King was not far away. The King comforted him through the night until the early hours of the morning, when one of the brothers returned. Guilt now filled the once jealous brother. He retrieved Nadav from the pit and sold him to a merchant who was passing by on his way to Egypt.

"A merchant who just happened to be passing by on is way to Egypt," Konnory whispered. "There is an entire universe working to bring them back. Balbas is correct. If they only could realize it, their lives would be so different."

Nadav was transported to Egypt in chains and sold as a slave. Nadav found favor with the man who purchased him, and in a very short time, he was given authority over all the man owned.

From the beginning, the lady of the house had a fascination for Nadav, but with wisdom and direction, he avoided her advances. Angered by his consistent refusal, she seduced him a final time. Again, Nadav refused and when he turned to leave, she caught his jacket and tore it from him. With evidence in hand, the lady of the house accused Nadav of raping her. Nadav was sent to prison and, there again, he called out to his King.

Nadav never forgot the King. Even in the seclusion of prison, Nadav walked daily with him. The King protected and provided for Nadav. He found favor in the eyes of the guards, and Nadav was given special responsibilities.

Two of the prisoners Nadav was responsible for had dreams that greatly disturbed them. They wrestled with the meanings of these dreams but were unable to find any explanation that satisfied. Nadav heard of the dreams and asked each to retell them to him. He listened intently, and while meditating on each dream, the King gave him the translation.

Nadav interpreted the dreams to their perspective owners. To the first, he would soon be put to death. To the other, he would find favor and be released from prison. Within hours, the dreams became reality and as the second prisoner prepared for his release, Nadav requested that he inform the ruler of his ability to interpret dreams. The fellow prisoner assured him that he would.

Two years later, Nadav remained imprisoned. But he never stopped walking with the King.

"Father," Konnory spoke out loud, "I don't understand how you can have so much patience with the Humans. Why don't you jump in? Why don't you just make it happen? I guess that's why you are King and I'm sitting here next to a babbling brook reading your stories." He chuckled to himself, as he shifted his position and continued reading.

The ruler of the foreign land where Nadav had been imprisoned had a dream...

"Oh, so you were willing to wait two years but no longer..." Konnory smiled and went back to the beginning.

The ruler of the foreign land where Nadav had been imprisoned had a dream. No one was able to interpret it. Every advisor had been told the dream and each was unable to decipher its true meaning. It happened that a servant, two years released from prison, had a connection. He told the ruler of Nadav and his ability to interpret dreams. Nadav was immediately called for an audience.

The ruler once again shared his dream. Nadav listened intently. As the ruler described the dream, the King made it real in Nadav's mind. When the ruler finished, he stared down at Nadav. Nadav stood motionless. The ruler leaned forward and as he was about to call for Nadav to be removed from his presence. Nadav spoke, "Your dream is a fore shadowing of the future. Your land will experience great drought and desolation. Your crops will fail, your livestock will die, and your people will suffer greatly. However," Nadav raised his hand, "The King of the Universe will grant you equal years prior to prepare. He will bless your land and your crops will be abundant. Your livestock will be greatly multiplied and your people will store up for themselves provision to last to the end."

The ruler sat back. He rubbed his beard in a kingly manner. He knew in the depths of his soul that Nadav had delivered to him the exact meaning of his dream. The ruler ordered Nadav to be given all authority required to ensure his people and his land would survive what lay ahead of them.

Konnory again looked up from his reading. He recalled Father telling this very story one evening at dinner. Father was elated at the outcome. Konnory looked around, there was no sign of Waldemar, and the new walkway was coming along beautifully. Konnory went back to his reading.

Nadav became the second highest official in the land. The King was with him every step of the way. As promised, the land produced generously and the livestock multiplied a hundred fold. Storehouses were built to hold the extras for the years of hardship to come.

And come it did, just as Nadav said. The drought and desolation spread beyond the rulers domain. Daily, Nadav welcomed those from outside his control to share in the bounty they had stored up.

One afternoon as he welcomed and listened to the pleas for assistance, he recognized a small group of men waiting in line. He couldn't keep his eyes off them. He knew them. But it couldn't be. As the line shortened and the men grew closer, Nadav found certainty that these were his brothers. Within a few minutes, they stood in front of him and bowed low. Nadav closed his eyes and replayed the dream he had so many years past. He became so filled with emotion that he had to take his leave.

From a back chamber, Nadav cried out to the King. The King listened as Nadav unloaded the years of pain he had carried. The King comforted and reassured. With a little coaxing, Nadav found the strength to return and face his brothers.

Upon his return, he greeted them as if they were strangers. None of them recognized him. Nadav questioned them about their land. Was their father alive? Were there other brothers at home?

The moment Nadav revealed himself to them, the brothers were filled with fear. What they had done was unforgivable. But Nadav understood forgiveness and freely offered it to his brothers. Nadav was reunited with his father and was able to provide for all his family for the remainder of their lives.

Konnory turned the page. The heading read: DETAILED DESCRIPTION OF LIFE. The word FORGIVEN was stamped across the page. Konnory smiled. "Details have no importance once forgiveness is found," he said.

He closed the file and was reaching for the next as Waldemar set a small serving table next to him. "I trust this will suffice?" he asked.

"It is perfect," Konnory replied.

Chapter Fourteen

Time had never been important in the Kingdom until the creation of Turayn. In Turayn, time controlled and measured every aspect of life. The Human form was so frail it required daily rest to repair and strengthen. It also required regular nutrition for health. A day in Turayn moved quickly and provided the Human with sufficient time for work and rest. It was estimated that a day in the Kingdom equaled one hundred years in Turayn. This was only an estimation, as time had never needed to be measured in the Kingdom.

Each new morning in the Kingdom equaled five generations in Turayn. Each morning was filled with new stories and increased numbers of the redeemed.

Jael was a few minutes late for breakfast. As he made his way through the corridors of the castle greeting the servants, he could hear Father's excited voice echoing from the Dining Room. Jael entered as the Queen was taking her leave. His mind flashed back to when Tayten would come to collect the Princes for their studies. It was so good to have Tayten back. Jael was reminded that it was Mother's routine to say, "Have a kingly day!" as the young Princes would take their leave. Tayten had encouraged them to respond by wishing their mother to have the same. "And a queenly day to you!" the young men would respond. As the images played over in his head, he was laughing as he greeted the Queen.

"What is so funny this morning?" she asked.

"Oh – nothing," he answered, as he leaned in to give her a kiss. He just couldn't help it, "Have a kingly day!" he said.

"Shouldn't that be Queenly day?" Mother asked.

"Yes, if you were the Queen, but these days you're the King!" Jael saluted.

The Queen laughed, "I guess you are right," she hesitated, "a kingly day to you as well!" She leaned in closer and lowered her voice. "Your Father is talking about Hadad. All Konnory had to do was bring up his name. He loved that boy so. It was almost as if Konnory was back in Turayn."

"I don't recall Him speaking of Konnory in such detail," Jael said. The Queen made her way down the hall surrounded by attendants. Jael entered the Dining Room.

As he entered, the King paused for a moment acknowledging his entry. Jael saluted, breaking a smile in the King's intensity. He quickly regained his concentration and continued. "He was such a good chap. As a lad, he had a strong nature, very confident, very confident indeed. He tended his father's sheep you remember? He was brave, even killed a few beasts that were trying to attack his flock. He reminded me of you, Jael."

"Father, wasn't he just a boy?" Jael replied, as he walked over to the serving table.

"Ah yes, just a boy. I do enjoy a child who seeks forgiveness at a young age. Don't misunderstand, they are all fascinating, but there is something about a child: endless energy, an endless flow of ideas, questions, and plans. At times, I've thought we may have made a mistake by allowing the Humans to grow up so quickly," said the King.

"If there were only children, who would teach them? Children left alone can be very destructive," said Jael. With a filled plate, Jael took his seat at the table.

"I am well aware of that fact. I would say, I know it firsthand," The King said, as he looked around the table at each son. Magnor laughed first, remembering the great adventures he had not only instigated but lured his brothers into.

The King finished his last few bites of breakfast and pushed his chair back to continue his story. "One day, this lad's father sent him on a journey to visit his brothers who were serving in battle. There he was, young Hadad weighed down with bread and cheese for his brothers, making his way to the battlefield all alone. He arrived just in time to witness a soldier from the other side making threats. Out in the field was this big beast of a man, he was yelling threats, he accused them of being weak.

Because of his size and strength, the opponents challenged the army to send but one warrior out to fight. The winner of the skirmish would be the victor."

Magnor laughed, "A battle being fought by two warriors. Seems like a waste of training to me."

"Hadad listened intently to the threats and with great anticipation waited for his brothers' army to attack. But no one did. He questioned his brothers but was ignored - as most older brothers do." The King paused giving Magnor a fatherly glance. "He could not believe there was no one willing to fight. Boldly he walked up to the commander and offered to accept the challenge. They let him!" the King said slapping his hand on the table. "What a sight to behold! They took him to their king, who really turned out to be quite a disappointment. He could have been so great. You never can tell can you?"

"You're the one who said they should have Free Will. It would have been much easier..." Ferrul chimed in.

"That is not open for discussion!" The King continued, "They tried to outfit the lad in warrior gear. The poor thing couldn't move. He put forth great effort but couldn't even walk across the room with it. The sword they gave him was bigger than he was. He had great strength for a child his age but to lift a sword of that size, it was impossible. They encouraged him to keep it on, that he would get used to it. After a few more attempts, he set down the sword, took off the armor and graciously told the king he would be unable to use them because they were not yet tested.

"Hadad straightened his tunic, checked in his pocket for his sling shot and stones, then headed back out to the field. The commanders walked behind him as he passed the hundreds of soldiers standing on the sidelines, dressed in armor, and shaking in fear.

"That lad walked right out to the middle of the field. The opponent yelled jests to the boy, but he kept on walking. Without hesitation, he shouted out, 'I come in the name of the King. On this day you will see his power. With great confidence and amazing calm, he placed one of the stones from his pocket into the sling and whispered softly, 'I do this in Your name'. Well, that's all I needed to hear. That stone flew with the power and accuracy of a hundred Watchers."

"Is that how many were there?" Konnory asked.

"Just about," the King replied with a smirk. "We all watched as that beast of a man went lifeless and then fell like a tree in the forest. The ground shook when he hit. Then, you'll never believe this! Hadad walked up to the lifeless body – it must have been six times his size – picked up the brute's sword – dear child could barely hold it – and cut off that monster's head - right there in front of everyone. Put those other warriors to shame, he did. Next, he picked up the head – almost as big as he was – and marched to the city, right up to the palace and handed the head to the king. He showed them all that day!"

"Sounds like someone you should meet," Konnory said, looking at Magnor.

"Sounds like someone I trained!" replied Magnor. "Father, what's come of this mighty hero?"

"He grew into quite a man, a mighty warrior. Come to think of it, he never lost a battle. You could have trained him, Magnor." The King motioned for the servant to bring more fruit to the table. "One of the finest battles I recall was in the Valley of Ziglor."

"Ziglor? Who comes up with these names?" Magnor asked.

"I didn't," Konnory replied. "Blame me for naming the animals but cities, the Humans created those."

The King continued on, "Hadad and his warriors were engaged in battle with an evil ruler, there's plenty of those in Turayn. While they were gone, another army entered their camp, took the women, children and all their possessions. When Hadad returned, he and his warriors were consumed with anger and sorrow. After days of grieving their loss, a young boy entered the camp. He was weak and sickly, and they took pity on him. When he regained his strength and was able to speak, Hadad asked him how he found himself alone in the wilderness. The boy had been a servant to one of the officers who attacked Hadad's camp! Can you believe it? The boy became ill and they left him behind."

"The boy just happened to become ill and was left behind?" Ferrul questioned.

"Yes! That's exactly how it happened!" The King said reassuringly. "Hadad and I talked about his options. He never went into a battle without consulting Me. I loved that about him! He became so very dear to me. He asked for permission to attack, and I gave it without reservation. After all, there was no doubt that Patho had his hand in all of it. The boy showed Hadad where the army was camped. Hadad attacked and took back all that had been stolen from him. Everything! Not one of the women or children were harmed!" the King said with great satisfaction.

"How is it possible that no one was harmed?" Magnor questioned.

"Watchers," replied the King.

The King now had Ferrul's full attention. "What do you mean, Watchers? Have you been reassigning them again?"

"Some," said the King. "I have established a regiment of Watchers who are equal in their strength and wisdom to the Warriors who protect Turayn. At times, there arises a need to assign them to special situation. This was a special situation." Ferrul took a deep breath and returned to his work. He didn't see any real harm in the King's plan and even if he did, he wasn't sure it was a battle he wanted to fight.

Konnory broke the tension, "Did he remain a warrior?"

"No, they made him king. He was my very own protégé," said the King.

"Father, what do you mean? More Watchers?" asked Jael.

"No. Watchers were not required for this one," said the King. They waited for further explanation but there would not be one.

"How did he do as King?" Carasi asked.

The King sighed, "Fine, fine, yes indeed. He did quite fine."

"Quite fine?" questioned Magnor hearing reservation in Father's answer.

"Well, there were a few bumps along the road. Patho had gotten very good at pitting people against temptation. He made his mistakes, and they weren't little ones," the King paused reflecting on Hadad's life. "But he earnestly sought forgiveness each time. He had the heart of a king." The King sat back in his chair. The brothers could sense the King's love for Hadad.

"Father, do you believe that Hadad could have been our answer? Was he strong enough to have ensured that all Humans would seek forgiveness?" Konnory asked, as he looked at the King.

There was a silence in the room. The mood had quickly changed. "No," the King replied, "Hadad was not the one." No more was said.

Chapter Fifteen

Time had passed and Hadad's life in Turayn had come to an end. The King had watched over Hadad until his last day. There was great hope and excitement in the Kingdom about the return of Hadad, but no one was able to locate the information revealing just who Hadad was in the Kingdom.

The King was just as fond of Hadad's son, Jair, as he had been of Hadad. Jair had a special place in the King's heart. The King knew Jair from the day he was born. He and the King were quite a pair.

Jair was eager to learn. He wanted to experience life to its fullest. His wisdom was unmatched. There was nothing that Jair couldn't understand, nothing he was afraid to question. Jair grasped the most integral details, and in doing so, found even greater wisdom. His curiosity delighted the King.

The King sat at the head of the table and as the meal was ending, he leaned back in his chair, recalling recent events in Turayn. "He is so inquisitive," said the King.

"Who is Father?" Jael asked.

"Jair wants to know everything. Today, we spent the day discussing the water cycle and the wind. The wind! He has such insight, yet he can pick out the simplest things. It's just delightful. You know he had a visitor last week?"

"Who?" Jael asked again.

"Jair, of course," The King responded. "It was the Human queen, the one who thinks she doesn't need forgiveness because of all her charm. She was impressed with dear Jair's riches and even more so with his wisdom. Dear fellow, I enjoy spending time with him so very much."

"Who?" Konnory asked.

The King realized he did not have his son's full attention. He continued, "There was this incident where two women came to him. Jair is an amazing judge; such wisdom, such insight. Both of these women were claiming to be the mother of one child. Jair wasted no time. He ordered the child to be cut in two, so the women could each have half the child. The guards did as Jair commanded and handed half a child to each one."

Carasi had just taken a drink and began to choke. An attendant rushed to his side.

"He did what!?" Magnor asked almost jumping out of his seat.

"He cut the child in half!?" Ferrul said, as he slammed his hands on the table. "What is happening to that place?"

"He couldn't have!" said Konnory. "You watched this happen?"

The King paused, settled back in his chair, folded his arms, and with a nod said, "No, the child was not cut in two. But let that be a lesson to you boys, I am still King and if I so desire - I can have five sons who don't feel the need to give me their attention, or I can have ten half sons who do!" The princes burst into laughter. The King had made his point. He had their attention.

Waldemar entered the Dining Room. It was obvious that he was uneasy. He was holding a file in his hand.

Those who returned to the Kingdom were expected to complete a proving time. It was a time designed for growth and development. A time used for instruction and opportunities for maturity. It was a time of testing and training, there were no exceptions.

Waldemar accepted his proving time with open arms. Everything changed on the day he left the Kingdom with Patho. He now understood about choices, options, disobedience, the need for repentance, and most of all, forgiveness. He was in no hurry to resume his former position. In fact, he was very content being a servant. It was an honor for him to serve his King in any manner. During his proving time, he was assigned personal service to the King, and he did it with the highest level of integrity. Perhaps even a higher level than his previous post as a warrior.

"Sire, I have some information that I believe You..." he paused, turning his attention toward Magnor, "...that all of you will be interested in."

"Sit, Waldemar," encouraged The King, motioning to the empty chair next to him.

"I'd rather not, Sire. This is of great..." Waldemar looked around the room, seeing that the servants were at a standstill, as they had sensed the seriousness of the moment and were waiting for an appropriate time to begin working again. "Please, everyone, I ask that you leave us. You can come back and finish your tasks shortly." With that, the attendants left what they were doing and made their way to the door.

Waldemar looked down at the folder that he tightly held, he opened it and removed the first page. "It has been brought to my attention that someone has made it home. In fact, they have been here for some time but have been somewhat in hiding."

"Hiding? Why? Who? There is no need for hiding in this Kingdom. Out with it! Of whom do you speak?" Magnor was on his feet.

Waldemar hesitated, almost unable to get the words out. He had spent the entire day practicing his speech and now, it was as if he hadn't given it a thought. He cleared his throat in hopes it would help. It did not. Forcing out each word he finally began, "It's Odella." Waldemar's voice cracked as he said her name. Magnor fell to his chair. Jael reached out to catch him.

"Waldemar, are you sure? How do you know this? How long has she been here?" Ferrul asked jumping out of his chair and making a beeline to Waldemar's side. "Give me the report." Waldemar handed him the file. "How long has she been here?" Ferrul scanned though the dates on the pages. "That's impossible." Ferrul read through the information as quickly as he could.

Carasi leapt from his chair and almost bounded across the table but thought it best not to. Within seconds, he was standing behind Ferrul trying to read the report as well. "How could she have gone unnoticed?" he asked, looking over Ferrul's shoulder.

Konnory got up from the table and made his way to the door. Opening it, he caught the attention of someone in the hall. "Please, call Mother. She would want to be here."

"Yes, Sir." The attendant bowed and hurried off. Konnory returned to his seat. Ferrul and Carasi were frantically reading through the report. Magnor was sitting motionless in his seat with Jael close beside him. Waldemar stood next to the King, like a young child who had just been found out.

"Odella." Magnor whispered her name. Magnor was not one to show weakness. He was a warrior. His brothers had not seen him this vulnerable since the day he received the news she had left.

Odella had been the most beautiful woman Magnor had ever beheld. He would lose himself in her deep brown eyes. She had a small frame—small but in no way frail. Magnor knew her strength. She had spent time with him while he trained. He knew her physical strength matched her intelligence.

Odella and Magnor had been introduced during an early inspection of the troops. It was just shortly after the King had promoted him to his current position. He was confident, yet hesitant, of this great responsibility. Odella seemed to know how to calm his fears. From the moment they met, he was smitten.

The bold, straightforward way in which he commanded authority did not last when he was in Odella's presence. Magnor felt as if he turned back into a young boy, wanting to run in the field and jump from rock to rock as he crossed the river. Odella did that to him. The most exciting part of their relationship was that Magnor knew if he did go running through the field or jumping on the rocks, Odella would be right by his side, enjoying every moment. She was his love, she was his joy, and she was his everything. They had courted for some time before Magnor got up the nerve to ask for her hand in marriage. When she left, a part of him died.

"From what I am told, she is humbled," Waldemar began. "She barely resembles her former self. She requested to be placed as the lowest servant in the court of the groundskeeper. She felt she had done so much to destroy the Kingdom, and you Sir," looking at Magnor, "that all she wanted to do, was in some way be a part of bringing beauty to her beloved home."

"Why were we not informed when she arrived?" asked Jael.

"She requested that her arrival not be announced." Waldemar turned his attention to the King. "Not that every request is granted, Sire, but the Kingdom knows the heartache and pain she caused Magnor and everyone else when she left. No one was sure how to handle it. It was brought to my attention last evening. After pacing the floor through the night, I knew it was not only my duty, it was the honorable thing to make her presence known to you."

"Thank you, my friend." These were the first words the King had spoken. Odella was the first woman, besides the Queen, who had successfully won the hearts of everyone in that room. Many had tried. The King had countless visits from fathers who believed their daughters would meet the requirements and obligations required of a Princess. The King had watched Magnor and Odella's relationship from the start. On the day they met, the King was at Magnor's side during the inspection. He recalled their meeting vividly. Odella's beauty, strength, and dignity were unmatched. The King could not have found anyone more suited for his son. Besides that, their love for each other was immeasurable. When the news arrived that she had left, it ripped a hole in all of them.

The King turned to Magnor. "There are no expectations here. You do as you see fit. There is no doubt we all loved Odella. On the morning we were informed of her leaving, it was devastating to all of us. But you, son, have carried the loss and pain of losing your betrothed. There is no pain its equal."

The room fell silent. There was only an occasional word whispered as Ferrul and Carasi read through the report.

Konnory made his way to the window and was gazing out over the beautiful gardens. He could not help but think Odella may have been working in the flowerbeds all this time. Had she put the orange and purple flowers together? Was it she that dug through the soil, removing imperfection in the gardens? Odella won Magnor's heart, but she had also won a special place in each of the Princes' hearts as well. She was like a sister to them.

Suddenly, there was a loud gasp, and papers fell to the floor. Waldemar slowly turned toward Ferrul and Carasi, "You saw it?" Waldemar asked.

Carasi covered his mouth; he and Ferrul were both speechless. They looked at each other, then to Waldemar, to Magnor, to the King, and back at each other. For a moment, they were unable to breathe. Carasi began to beat his chest with his hand as if trying to gasp for air. Both were flooded with memories— not memories from long ago, but of recent stories Father had shared during dinner. Stories of battles, of mighty warriors, of glorious kingdoms, of dancing in the street and of beautiful music played on a harp. Of this person the King had such high hopes, the Human that had won the heart of the King—the one who the King enjoyed being with so often. They began to chuckle, and then laugh. It was a laughter that took over total control of their beings. Both knew it was an inappropriate response at such a delicate time, but neither could hold back.

"What? What is it?" Konnory demanded.

In the midst of the laughter, Ferrul and Carasi squeaked out the words, "Tell them! You tell them!" they ordered, as they waved their hands wildly towards Waldemar.

"Waldemar, what is it man? What has these two imbeciles laughing at such a time?" the King bellowed, as he rose from the chair.

"Sire, I don't know if I can even speak it." There was great reluctance in Waldemar's voice. It felt as if hours were passing. Again, he found himself struggling to get each word out. "The time Odella spent in Turayn, she...she...she was..."

"Who?" shouted Konnory now on his feet leaning across the table.

"She was...Hadad!" both Ferrul and Carasi shouted in unison.

"NO!" shouted Konnory in disbelief and fell back into his chair. "Hadad?"

"Yes," replied a very wide-eyed Ferrul.

"Hadad?" the King said. "My Hadad? The lad...the sheep? The kid...the sword...the giant's head? The mighty warrior... who never lost a battle?" He looked at Magnor in disbelief. "The warrior you could have trained? The king who danced in the streets? Odella!? How could this be? I never thought, never dreamed he was...her."

The King glanced at the door and realized that the Queen was standing there. "Have you heard?" He asked softly.

"Yes," she said ever so gently.

There was something in her tone and simple answer that made the King inquire, "When?"

"A day ago," she replied. The Queen made her way to the King's side. As she passed Konnory and Jael, she placed her hand on each one's shoulder as a way of comforting them. To Magnor, she bent over and gently kissed his forehead. He sat motionless in the chair with Jael by his side. When she reached the end of the table, she stood next to the King and placed her hand on his arm. "But I knew it," she said directly to the King. The room was silent and the air heavy. Looking around the room at the confusion and befuddlement of each one she continued, "Waldemar is correct, she barely resembles her former self. I've been watching her. I suspected it might be her. Yesterday, it was confirmed."

"Why..." Jael began. Mother put her hand up to quietly stop him.

"Magnor," she said in a loving whisper, "she was your love." Looking at each of her other sons, she called them by name, "Konnory, Jael, Carasi, Ferrul, she became a sister to you all. Odella had become a daughter to me. When I lost her, it was almost as difficult as losing Palti and Quaine. I needed time; I needed to know that it was truly her."

"When were you going to say something?" Magnor asked. One would have expected his tone to be angry, but it wasn't. He was in a state of shock.

"Who do you think gave the file to Waldemar?" she said, with her gentle and all knowing smile. She squeezed the King's arm, "Now, I know why you loved him so. I guess you didn't lose your Hadad." The King smiled for the first time since Waldemar had entered the room with the news. She leaned in and gently kissed him.

The Queen ever so gracefully made her way to Waldemar. Waldemar's face showed signs of a sleepless night and stress filled day. She reached down and took his hands in hers. Waldemar looked up. Her eyes saw to the core of his very being. "You did the right thing," she said very reassuringly.

"I wasn't sure," Waldemar said. "I paced all night." Waldemar's head dropped to one side.

"I know," the warmth of her smile radiated through the room. "One of the guards on patrol last night informed me he heard footsteps through the night. He figured you could have walked to Turayn and back."

Waldemar laughed softly. He had forgotten just how beautiful she was. He knew of her strength, her ability to command an audience. But it was her depth of wisdom that he had not noticed before he left the Kingdom. "If I may," Waldemar began. All his fear and apprehension were gone. Standing in the Queen's presence was like standing in a sphere of complete peace. "Why was I the lucky one to be given the file?"

"Because you need to..." the Queen stopped. She gently squeezed his hands. He could feel her warmth and strength. She leaned into him and for a moment, it was if no one else in the room existed. "You needed to remember," she said. "And you do remember, don't you?"

"Yes...yes, I do," Waldemar replied. He could not help but smile as his eyes began to fill with tears. He, too, had known Odella. She had changed Magnor's world. She was his love. She had somehow found a way into the heart of these men and this woman. Like the Queen, Odella did not need anyone to take care of her, yet each of them wanted to.

Waldemar also knew what it was like outside the Kingdom. He knew the pain of the great separation from the King. He hadn't allowed himself to do so until this very moment, but imagining this beautiful child
wandering out in the emptiness and the Darkness flooded him with emotion. He remembered. How could he ever forget? The King, Queen, and Princes had experienced and could feel her loss, but he knew her suffering.

Chapter Sixteen

Reeturning from Turayn, the King walked through the garden on the way to the castle. He saw Konnory sitting next to the stream, a stack of files next to him. The King made a detour to join him. "Who is next?" he asked.

"I've not decided on the next one."

The King looked down at the files, "How did you choose these? They are out of order," said the King.

"No one explained their order," answered Konnory. "I took files of names that looked interesting."

The King reached down and grabbed a file. "Lior! You have to hear about Lior, one of the bravest prophets we've had."

"If I recall, there was some question about how he got home," said Konnory.

The King put his head back and laughed. Konnory waited, hoping there would be an explanation, but as was becoming more and more frequent, none came. Konnory reached out to take the file, but the King did not relinquish it.

The King opened the file and scanned its contents. "Have you seen her?" he asked without looking up.

Konnory smiled. "No, I've been hoping that I would either notice her or she would come to me."

"We'll have to wait," the King replied.

"When she's ready," Konnory said. Both took a deep breath that did very little to relieve their anticipation.

"Lior was fearless," began the King, making a quick end to their conversation. "And he was willing to do anything I suggested. He didn't look like a great warrior. He was quite small in fact. There was nothing in his demeanor that shouted 'Watch out, here I come!' But when he came, people noticed.

"There was a time that I actually thought it would be best for Lior to go into hiding. He did not simply have one ruler after him, he had several. I arranged for a bird to deliver his daily food. Every day the bird would land just outside the cave, where we had secluded him with a small package of supplies. On occasion, I sent a few delicacies from the Kingdom which delighted him greatly. He was a great partner."

"You arranged for his seclusion?" Konnory asked.

"It was either me or one of the Watchers. They are a capable group. The Watchers and Messengers are becoming quite creative."

"I'm sure Balbas adds his opinions."

"Balbas! It's a good thing that one is surrounded by Watchers and Messengers. He's capable of getting into trouble with some of his plans."

"Has he met Magnor?" Konnory asked.

"Heaven's no!" the King replied. "Magnor and his trees and Balbas and his scheming, may those two never meet."

"That would probably be best," Konnory jest.

"But I want to tell you about Lior. There was a ruler that did everything possible to get the Humans to believe in other gods. I encouraged Lior to challenge him. Both sides would build altars, they to their gods and Lior to me. The plan was that without any assistance in starting the fire, whichever altar would start burning due to the prayers offered, that alter would be the altar of the true King.

"So the ruler built his elaborate altar and spent the day surrounded by his advisors. They danced and shouted to their gods in hopes that his altar would burn. Lior and I watched. By evening, Lior was so riled up, he started yelling at the other group, 'Shout louder, maybe no one is listening!' Several times he stood up and began mimicking the advisors which drew cheers from the crowd.

"By nightfall the ruler and his followers were exhausted and gave up the effort, but we were just getting started." The King rubbed his hands together in anticipation. Konnory couldn't help but notice the excitement in the King's eyes. "All I said was, 'Let's prove to them once and for all the power of the true King!' And he was off!

"Lior got the attention of the crowd once again. 'I need your assistance,' he shouted. 'It appears the altar and wood are dry. I need water to be brought and poured over it.' This was a crowd pleaser! The people lined up with every empty container they could find. They formed a line and dumped gallons upon gallons of water over the altar making the chance that it would burn almost nonexistent. The stage was set—all eyes were on him. Unlike the pompous display put on by the ruler and his advisors, Lior quietly bowed his head and said, "Prove your power today."

"That's all I needed to hear. I motioned for him to step back, way back! This wasn't going to be a little flame. Flames shot out from every crack and crevice. In fact, the fire was so hot, the stones burned. It was well into the night when the fire died, nothing was left of the sacrifice or the altar. Lior won the attention of the ruler that night. However, as rulers can be, this one was arrogant and proud; it would take more than fire coming down from the sky to make him seek forgiveness.

"After many years of battles, adventures, and human rulers, I was eager to get him home," the King paused.

"I remember our dinner conversation that night," Konnory said. "Ferrul had asked if you were aware of any out-of-the-ordinary events in Turayn. You looked at Mother and smirked. Then you looked back at us and said, 'No, nothing that I wasn't aware of.' It was a smirk like you have right now." The King began to laugh. "Carasi said that there were chariots sent and there was a charge in the atmosphere."

"I couldn't bring him home as I had done with Waldemar. You had all made that very clear," the King responded.

"Right, as if we could change your mind," Konnory said. "How did you bring him home?"

"It was all very natural. There was wind, thunder, and fire – and he was home."

"That sounds very natural to me," Konnory said with a smirk that resembled that of the King's.

Konnory picked up the remaining files. "Who else is in there?" asked the King. Konnory fanned them out.

"Ram!" He said with great excitement. Konnory found the file, and opened it. "Ram was a great friend," the King began. "We talked three times a day.

"Ram was a strong leader and because of his honesty and straightforwardness, he found great favor with the Human ruler he served. This made the ruler's advisors very jealous. They decided he needed to dispose of him. They tricked the ruler into making a decree requiring all to worship him and him alone.

"Ram could not honor such a demand even knowing it would result in death. When all this was brought to the ruler's attention, he knew immediately that he had been scammed. There was nothing he could do. The law had been written and sealed in such a way that even he could not change it. Reluctantly, the ruler had Ram thrown into a den of lions as was required by the decree. The den was sealed with a large boulder. The ruler spent the night agonizing over the events of the day. It must have been a sleepless night for him," said the King.

"Father," Konnory rubbed his chin as he recalled an unusual night. "If I recall, it was a sleepless night for many." The King was suddenly quiet. "Rumor had it that there was quite a party that night. That was the night Mother, Waldemar, and you could not be found."

"Interesting," said the King. "You're not suggesting–"

"I don't think I need to suggest," said Konnory. "You know what happened."

"Yes, I do," said the King with kingly confidence. "The next morning, Ram was safe and sound in the den with the lions."

"I guess when the Creator says, 'Sit, don't bite,' even the king of beasts obeys," Konnory said.

"There are many rulers who could learn such a lesson," said the King. "After Ram was safely removed from the den, the ruler questioned how he survived. Ram said a Messenger from the true King had been there to close their mouths."

"A Messenger?" Konnory laughed. "How did the ruler respond?" he asked.

"He was angry, as he should have been," said the King. "He had been deceived and manipulated. He had all of his advisors who participated in this plot thrown into the same den."

"Was there another party?" asked Konnory.

"Only for the lions," said the King. "Law of Consequence took care of it."

Chapter Seventeen

Is this a private conversation, or may I join?" came a voice from behind them.

Konnory immediately stood, "Mother, of course you can join. You may be able to fill in the gaps that Father seems to be forgetting."

"I very much doubt that," said the Queen. "Are these a new collection of stories?" The Queen looked over the files.

"Yes. They are so used to me coming down now that they have a new stack waiting for me when I arrive," answered Konnory. "They've even set up a table for me, but I much prefer reading out here."

"Are you sure all you are doing is reading?" Mother asked.

The King leaned in and whispered, "Do you see her?"

The Queen glanced across the gardens, "No, I don't believe she is here."

"If she was," Konnory began, "would you tell us?"

"Most likely not," She said. "Odella will make herself known when she is ready. Now, whose file do you have?" the Queen asked. The King turned the file around. "Ada, you loved that one!" she said with a glowing smile. "You and the children," the Queen turned her attention back to Konnory. "When children seek forgiveness, it melts your Father's heart."

"Who is this Ada?" Konnory asked.

"She was a lovely young thing," said the Queen. "She had been orphaned and lived with her uncle. He was a gentle soul. She could not have been more loved and cared for. He knew her beauty and character were rare, and when the king announced he was looking for a new queen, Ada's uncle signed her up.

"Ada applied herself, she learned from the others, she found great favor with those who watched over the young women. When she was summoned by the king, he was taken with her beauty and character and thereby proclaiming her to be his next queen.

"Ada's uncle stayed as close as he could to her. He spent most of his days in the palace courtyard hoping to catch word of his loved one. While in the courtyard, he overheard a plan to kill the king being devised by some of the guards, and he got word to Ada to inform the king. Ada does so, the king investigates and finds out it was true. He then has his recorders write this all down in his book of records."

"Remember that," the King said pointing to Konnory, "She's going to come back to it."

"Let me finish?" the Queen asked.

"By all means," the King offered.

"The human king had a servant who was one of the most arrogant, self-centered human that there ever was. Somehow, the king kept promoting him until he had great power. This one had a disdain for anyone seeking forgiveness and decided he is going to rid his world of them. He begins to make his plans.

"Somehow, Ada's uncle once again heard of this plan and got word to Ada. He instructed her to tell the king immediately. But Ada questions her ability. She told her uncle that she would be risking her life by doing so. Her uncle lets her know in no uncertain terms, that his King will find a way to allow those seeking forgiveness to survive. It's up to Ada if she chooses to participate.

"Ada took time to consider and agreed to ask for an audience with the human king. In the meantime, she requested her uncle to gather as many friends as he could and for three days pray to the true King for guidance.

"Did they?" Konnory asked.

"Of course!" replied the King. "For three days, thousands of those who had been seeking forgiveness, fasted and prayed."

"You had great conversations with them, didn't you?"

"Ask your Mother," the King replied. "This was all her doing."

"You?" directing his attention to the Queen. "I thought you didn't get involved with Turayn and those Humans?"

"Ada was a special case," said the Queen.

His entire life, Konnory had heard his entire life that the King and Queen were one. He had seen glimpses of their oneness as a boy. When Mother took over the workings of the Kingdom for Father, no one really knew the difference. These two gracefully passed responsibility and authority between each other effortlessly. Each was their own person. He knew that for a fact, but he was beginning to see just how much they worked as one.

"And to answer your question, we did have great conversations during this time. Ada and I came up with a game plan."

"It was brilliant!" the King interjected.

"She was fearful. We had high hopes that she would follow through, but with the Human, you're never sure until the end. As each day passed, Ada's confidence grew. At the end, she said with great boldness, 'If I parish, then I parish.'" The Queen paused. "She couldn't fail!"

"You would make sure of that," said the King. "If you think I overdo it with Watchers and Messengers, you should have seen the army your Mother had prepared to surround Ada. If that girl had known, with her determination and your Mother's protection, she could have taking over the kingdom."

"What happened?" Konnory said. He had suddenly been transported back to his childhood listening to Mother and Father telling stories in front of the fire.

"Ada played the part perfectly. She began early in the morning preparing herself. She selected the finest gown."

"It was lavender as I recall," offered the King.

Mother nodded. "Her jewels sparkled in the sunlight. She had gathered an array of flowers that she held in one arm and draped a shawl over the other. She took her place just outside the entrance to the room where the king sat upon the throne. Ada waited. She was radiant. It took only moments for the king to notice her presence and invite her in."

Out of the corner of his eye, Konnory caught a glimpse of Father, who was now completely engulfed in the Queen's storytelling. Without prompting, he took on the role of the Human king, "What is your request?" he asked playing the part. "You shall have all you wish including half my kingdom."

"I only wish to invite you to a feast, and I would ask that you bring your highest officials as well," the Queen said playing the role of Ada.

"The following day the king and his court celebrated with Ada. As the feast came to an end, the king once again asked Ada what she desired. She simply said that she would so love to feast with the king and his men the following day."

"Here's where it gets good!" Father said. The Queen chuckled at how the King delighted in great stories.

"That night, Ada's king was unable to sleep," the Queen continued.

"I wonder why?" the King said. He was wide eyed and grinning with excitement.

"Hush now, let me tell the story. The king was having difficulty sleeping so he asked for a reading from his journal. The servant opened the large ledger and began reading."

"He just happened to open it to the story where Ada's uncle had informed him of the plan to murder him," the King said. "She is brilliant! Your Mother is just brilliant!"

"Ada's king recalled the story and realized that he had not rewarded Ada's uncle for his heroics. The next morning, he called for the highest ranked officer in his command."

"This is the one who was making plans to kill all seeking forgiveness?" Konnory asked.

"Yes, the very same," continued the Queen. "The night before, this officer had finished making the plan for the gallows he would use to eliminate all forgiveness seekers. As dawn broke, he received the summons from the king. When he arrived, the king asked, 'What would be an appropriate reward to honor someone who had done a great deed for the king?'"

"Of course, he assumed that Ada's king was referring to himself," the King interrupted. "So he lays out this prestigious plan. He says to put the man on the kings best horse, to dress him in the finest robes, give him the kings ring and parade him around the kingdom."

"Would you like to finish the story?" the Queen asked.

"Oh, no," the King said shaking his head, "You are doing a fine job."

"Thank you," the Queen replied. "As Ada's king heard the plan, he immediately agreed and ordered that all of this be done to Ada's uncle with one addition, that his second in command escort him by leading the horse."

"NO!" Konnory said.

"YES!" said the King.

"He hated Ada's uncle. Wasn't it Ada's uncle that got him thinking of killing all those seeking forgiveness?"

"The very one," said the Queen. "He was furious. But he did it. Ada's uncle was dressed in the finest of the king's robes, given the king's ring and lead around the kingdom by the man who hated him the most. When the parade ended the commander made his way home. As he passed the gallows, his

J. G. Bruenning

anger increased and all he could think about was Ada's uncle hanging from them.

"As he entered his house, he was furious. He told his wife of the morning's happenings. To his surprise, she wasn't angered by it. Instead, she sat in deep thought. 'What are you thinking?' he yelled. 'Why aren't you angry?'"

"'Perhaps,' she said, 'perhaps we were wrong. If the true King is on the side of Ada's uncle, there is nothing we can do to stop him.'"

"'What!' he yelled. 'After all this time! All this planning!! Now you say there is nothing we can do?'"

"At that very moment, there was a knock on the door. It was a messenger from the king coming to escort him to Ada's celebration. The commander quickly brushed himself off and was escorted back to the palace.

"Ada had once again laid out a fabulous feast. She was stunning. A deep purple robe, lined with jewels and the finest gemstones in the kingdom. She wore a floral wreath as a crown and tiny flowers were pinned in her long hair. The celebration lasted most of the afternoon, and as she and her king sat side-by-side, he reached over and took her hand. He once again ask what she desired and that all she needed to do was ask and half of his kingdom would be hers."

"Here it comes!" the King said with great delight.

"Shh," Konnory said.

"The scene was set. Ada had done everything we had discussed. Her king was sitting next to her as she reclined on a beautiful white chaise. Ada put her hand over his and looked into his eyes. The room began to glow as the Messengers and Watchers filled every space.

"Ada began, 'There is a plan in place to rid your kingdom of all who seek forgiveness from the true King.'

"The king nodded. 'Yes, it is my commander who has set this plan in motion.'

"Ada glanced at the commander. Bringing her attention back to her king she said, 'I ask that you save my life.'"

"What?" asked the king.

"If you allow him to rid the kingdom of those seeking forgiveness from the true King, you will be putting a death sentence on me and my uncle as well."

"The king was beside himself. He leapt to his feet and darted out to the balcony to think. The commander didn't know what to do. His wife's words echoed through his head, 'Perhaps we were wrong. If the true King is on the side of Ada's uncle, there is nothing we can do to stop him.' The commander fell across Ada's feet and began pleading for forgiveness."

"Here it comes!" said the King leaning forward in great expectation.

"As Ada's king reentered the room, he sees his commander laying across Ada's feet, she remained reclined on the chaise. Ada's king believes the commander is attacking his queen!"

"Are you serious!" Konnory asked, as he began to laugh.

"Your Mother knows how to put a plan together," the King said.

"The king is beside himself. He orders the commander be taken immediately to the gallows he had prepared for Ada's uncle and be hung."

Konnory sat speechless. The King was still grinning in delight.

"Your Mother was brilliant on that one," said the King. "What a plan. Perfectly instigated. She single-handedly saved thousands who were seeking forgiveness. All she needed was a few purple gowns and a party."

"There was a bit more to it than just that," the Queen said.

"Indeed, indeed," said the King.

"Mother, that was brilliant." He reached out and took the file. "This one I'm reading again." He fanned through the file. A boyish grin began to replace the intensity from which he had been listening. "It seems to me that no king can resist a purple dress and a party," he said.

The King looked at him. The Queen let out a puff of laughter.

"Are you going to elaborate?" asked the King. Konnory had piqued his interest.

"It just seems to me that Mother has many purple dresses," he said, now with a full grin.

The Queen smiled. "What an observant son you have become," she said. "That purple dress caught the attention of Ada's king, and the rest is history."

"It's a history that will be told until the end of time in Turayn," said the King. He paused as his glance bounced between the Queen and Konnory. "Do you really have several purple dresses?"

The Queen and Konnory broke into laughter.

Chapter Eighteen

Generations in Turayn had passed since the time of Ram, Lior, and Ada. Life there had changed greatly, and not for the better. It was a dark and empty time in Turayn. The Pit had been busy and had successfully quieted any who boldly spoke of forgiveness. Patho and his warlords had many techniques to stop anyone who spoke of the need for it.

Sacrifice, which had once been the only way to find forgiveness, had become a ritual. Patho had introduced an endless supply of gods who all required sacrifice. Whether it was a banana, raven, your first born, or a thousand virgins, sacrifice was as commonplace as having a meal and was no longer about remembering the King's forgiveness.

When the King and Magnor had established the first regiment of warriors responsible for guarding Turayn, they knew that there would be risk. It was underestimated how much risk Patho would offer. The Pit ensured that these warriors were tempted by continual sales pitches written and designed by Patho himself. They were delivered by the best of the best temptress from the Pit. Patho never let up, but he never succeeded.

The warriors who surrounded Turayn were willing to sacrifice whatever the cost for its safety. They had all lost someone near to them on that devastating day when Patho left the Kingdom. They had now been witness to the return of the Fallen Souls.

It was easy to see the changes in those who had found their way home, they were different in so many ways. Most struggled with acceptance. Many questioned their right to be forgiven. Those that left with Patho did it, to some degree, out of ignorance. If one were to leave the Kingdom now to join Patho, they would be doing so with their eyes wide open.

Although it was not true, Patho made great to do about the huge numbers of souls that continued to leave the Kingdom. He raved about the millions in Turayn who would serve him and him alone. With great confidence, he spoke of those who were once part of the King's own inner circle that were now under his command. One could not be sure if Patho believed such things or if he was just using words for his own gain, but the truth of the matter was Patho was losing ground.

He had never quite figured out how or why the Humans showed up on Turayn, but it really didn't matter to him. He was under the impression the Humans were there for his taking, and according to his records, he was gaining new souls every second of every day.

Patho had not been informed that he had lost three of the five he was most proud of having deceived. His warlords felt it would be best not to offer such information. When, or more hopefully, if he found out, it would be dealt with at such time. Patho's pride accomplishments, Tayten, Waldemar and Odella were no longer included in his conquests. They had already found their way back to the Kingdom. This information was safely hidden in the bottom drawer of his advisors desk.

Jael was determined to redeem his two brothers. For Quaine, it was just a matter of time. He was out there seeking forgiveness. Surely his request had been processed and now all they could do was to wait until he arrived. As for Palti, no one had heard from him. No one knew where he was, and there seemed little hope of his return.

The Princes met frequently to discuss the current state of Turayn. They, too, felt this was a dark and different time there. They were continually talking through options and strategies. It felt as if The Plan had become stagnate, and they wanted desperately to ignite it again. Patho had prostituted the offering of a sacrifice and a change needed to be made. Their meetings were long and laborious. Occasionally, the King joined these discussions, but it was obvious to all of them that he was there as an observer, not a participant. He had become increasingly distant of late, and they wanted to know why.

The King spent countless hours in the lower levels of the castle talking with Balbas and listening to the stories the Messengers and Watchers had to offer. The rest of the time, he secluded himself in his chambers or walked with the Queen through the Gardens.

The Princes were in the Dining Room having yet another discussion concerning Turayn.

"Will anyone be able to have an effect?" Konnory questioned.

"At this point, I'm unsure," answered Carasi. "Perhaps it's time to bring it to an end."

The Dining Room had once again become a conference room. The attendants did their best to keep it clean and organized, but all they had control over were the serving pieces and place settings. It was becoming increasingly difficult for them to set the table due to the piles of notes and tablets, writing utensils, maps, lists and, ledgers that filled the table and side bars.

"Bring what to an end? The Plan or Turayn?" questioned Magnor. He looked worn. None of them could recall just how long they had been in this room.

"Quite possibly both," said Ferrul as he rubbed his forehead. He reached over and grabbed a stack of papers, but realizing that they weren't what he was looking for, tossed them aside adding to the already disheveled mess.

"We have the end planned out to the smallest detail. My men have trained extensively for that scenario," said Magnor. "When Jael summons the warriors..."

"If I summon," Jael corrected.

"When you summon the warriors, they will attack; Patho and his warlords will be captured, and Father will seal them in the Pit once and for all! Yes, we have been over that plan many times. But it's up to Jael to give the order." Magnor paused. "Jael, are you ready to end this?" Jael did not answer.

"And what about the Humans and the rest of the Fallen Souls?" asked Konnory. He, too, was showing signs of exhaustion.

"Those who continued seeking forgiveness will return to the Kingdom." Magnor explained. "Those who haven't will return to the Darkness, Patho will be sealed in the Pit, and the rest of the Fallen Souls will remain in the Darkness with no hope of redemption."

"That can't be how this ends," Konnory said. "All this effort and we're satisfied to leave countless Fallen Souls out in the Darkness for eternity? I don't believe, I can't believe that is what the end looks like."

"We have never known what the end looks like," Ferrul said, as he shuffled through another stack of forms. "We didn't write the ending, and if you recall, Father reserved that portion of The Plan and has not offered anyone insight as to what He will do. We have to maintain until he moves."

"Maybe he is waiting for us to come to our own conclusion that this is over," Magnor said. "Jael, speak the words and let's bring an end to it." There was a loud gasp and then crash just outside the window causing everyone in the room to jump. "Who was that?" Magnor ordered.

"What was that?!" asked Carasi jumping up and heading to the window.

"I have no idea," said Ferrul. The room took a collective sigh. "There has been someone working in the flowerbed just below this window for some time. I can't imagine what they are doing. Whatever it is, it seems to be taking too long."

"I've notice them also - despite it never looking like anything has actually been done," added Jael raising his brow.

Konnory was the least distracted by the commotion; wanting desperately to end what now seemed an endless discussion. Reaching for the carafe and filling his goblet, he leaned back in his chair. He couldn't get his head around what was going through the King's mind. He saw the eagerness in Magnor's face to bring The Plan to an end, and the seemingly frustration between Carasi and Ferrul, as life in Turayn was becoming increasingly uneventful.

There had been such high hopes that someone, anyone would rise to the top and effectively proclaim the forgiveness offered by the King. None of them were sure how it was going to happen, but they knew there would have to be a significant sacrifice that would bring the remaining Fallen Souls home. Hadad had been an option, but he was too Human. There had been many who successfully proclaimed the King's message of forgiveness, but not worthy to be the sacrifice. *What were they missing? What was Father keeping from them. Why was he so distant?* "Jael, do you really believe it is time to act?" Konnory asked.

The commotion that had been outside the window had suddenly ended and there remained an uneasy void. Jael hesitated for a moment. "I'm not sure." he said.

"There is something greatly troubling Father." Carasi offered. "Mother says not to worry, that we will know in time. But I wish I knew what it was."

They heard shouting chasing footsteps coming from the hallway. It was clearly Waldemar's voice. "You can't go in there! You...! There...!"

Suddenly, the door flew open. Standing in the doorway was a small form covered in dirt. "Please, I beg you! You cannot bring an end to it! You must continue. None of you understand what it's like..." Whatever had caused the distraction just a few moments ago was now standing in their presence. The fact that they were all approaching new levels of exhaustion no longer matter. Each was focused on the figure that stood in the doorway.

Waldemar entered the room panting. "I'm sorry my Lords," he said to the Princes. Turning to the figure he restated, "You cannot be in here. You must leave at once!" Waldemar pointed to the door.

"Wait!" said Jael rather forcefully and startling Waldemar. "What do you want?" Waldemar looked at Jael and then back at the figure. Glaring at her and still pointing towards the door, he waited for her response.

There was a moment of hesitation as this bold entrance now seemed awkward. With head bowed, the figure began to remove the soil stained gloves, it was obvious they had been used in the garden. The room stood quiet. Who was this one? From the outward appearance it seemed a stranger. But it wasn't. They all felt it. Its presence brought a familiarity and comfort to the room.

The figure hesitated and then slowly removed the cloth that was protecting and hiding its face. As the intruder looked up, there was a united gasp from each of the Princes and a loud thud from the far side of the room. Konnory jumped from his seat and ran over to where Magnor had been standing. He had fainted and was flat on his back.

"Odella," Jael whispered. Waldemar's arm dropped, and Carasi put down his pen.

Odella wiped the dirt from her face. "You cannot truly begin to understand what most of us have been through. You will never understand why we left." She wiped a tear that mingled with the dirt and ran down her cheek.

"During those final moments, there were some who hesitated for just a moment, but that's all that Patho needed. So many who were dragged into Patho's mob had only considered the option; it all happened so quickly there was no time to reason. He created such a commotion it brought a level of excitement that only perpetuated the anticipation that something great was happening. But most didn't realize the complete impact of their decision until we found ourselves outside the gate, exiled forever. After that, we were on our own. Left to ourselves to try to make sense of what had happened. Aside from the ones who chose to follow Patho into the Pit, we were all wandering aimlessly in the Darkness, confining ourselves to our own prisons of guilt and regret. I believe most of us would have let those things fully consume us if it hadn't been for Quaine."

Across the room, on the other side of the large table, Magnor was coming to. He looked up at Konnory and pulled him down by his collar. "Is she still here?" he whispered.

"Can you not hear her speaking?" asked Konnory kneeling down next to him, now face to face.

"Get me out of here!" he said in a demanding whisper.

"No!" said Konnory. "You're not getting out of this one; you have to face this."

Magnor looked up at him. "What are you talking about?!" he demanded.

"Magnor, Odella is the reason you've been ambivalent about The Plan from the beginning. You're the only one that doesn't see it. You can't hide or run away. You have to face her," Konnory whispered.

Magnor shook his head. He knew he was in no position to fight it out with Konnory, but he tightened his grip of Konnory's collar just the same. With a look of defeat he said, "Get me to a chair, any chair. BUT it had better be as far from her as possible."

Odella watched as Konnory helped Magnor to his feet and then over to a chair near the hearth. Magnor sat down, doing his best to appear in control. She had desperately wanted, and at the same time, hoped this moment would never happen. She had no words for him. There were none that seemed able to convey her grief and pain of losing him. He did not look up at her, but she could not take her eyes from him.

Waldemar walked towards her. She pulled her cloak tight and held it as if it were a shield. He placed his hand on her shoulder as he stood looking down at her. When she found the courage to meet his glance, she found love and understanding in his eyes. He felt her shoulders soften as tears began to flow. Waldemar took the scarf from her hand and wiped the muddy streams from her beautiful face. Konnory stood behind his brother and watched as Waldemar offered to take her soil covered coat.

Jael stretched out his hand, and Odella gently took it. The warmth of his skin, the softness of his touch, unleashed a lifetime of memories that she had not allowed herself to entertain. Jael led her to a chair next to the window. As she sat, the light caught her profile and radiated out from her. She glanced at Magnor, and for a single moment, their eyes met before he turned away.

"Waldemar, you understand," Odella continued. "We left the Kingdom. We abandoned the King." Waldemar's head dropped. "The guilt and fear were unbearable. Even though we knew we didn't deserve it, Quaine gave us hope that the King might forgive us." Odella looked out the window.

Magnor caught another glimpse of her. "After your request goes through, you are torn out of the Darkness and awaken on Turayn in what feels like a stranger's body. Konnory, you understand what life is like in Turayn. Each day is just a struggle to get through to the next. There are heartbroken mothers and fathers having to bury their children. Things taken for granted in the Kingdom, like food and water, can be a struggle to provide for your family there. In Turayn, sometimes the most difficult task is surviving long enough so you can ask for the King's forgiveness just one more day. There are still so many left-- you cannot end it yet!"

Jael knelt down next to her. "But it's out of control. Patho aims at anyone who is there, and anyone who speaks out is eliminated. He has corrupted everything! He has managed to turn Sacrifice into a ritual. He has distorted every practice intended for good. We see no way out," said Jael.

"Patho may have his control," Odella scanned the room, addressing each of the Princes including Magnor. "But you are greater than that," Odella said. "You are willing and able to defeat him!" A charge of energy vibrated through the room.

And there it was! This is why they loved her so. Odella always knew what to say. It never took her more than a few words. She could turn a few words into a battle cry. Magnor watched as the others began to discuss their options. Konnory was right-- she was the reason he had opposed the thought of The Plan. Was he angry at her? Was he afraid he would never see her again? Never seeing her again, how could he have lived with that reality? It would have meant she did not want to return and refused to seek forgiveness, or that The Plan had failed. It would have meant that he was unable to rescue her. He could not have lived with the guilt and loss. Magnor was not one to show or even admit that he had emotions. The real issue was his emotions. Magnor had avoided even thinking of Odella because of his fear of those emotions. Now, he was not only being forced to face them, he was facing Odella.

"I've been there. I understand the struggle that goes on within the Human mind," Odella began. "The Human is three parts. There is the mind, which Patho works endlessly to control. There is the heart that offers emotion. Most humans fight to find any joy or positive feelings. They are consumed with fear and guilt. Finally, there is the spirit. It's the spirit that can hear the King. It's the spirit that pursues forgiveness." Carasi was writing as quickly as Odella spoke.

"I believe the Human spirit is always seeking goodness, it's just overpowered by the mind and heart. Fear plays such an enormous part in how a Human lives their life." Odella had everyone's attention. "But they are all searching, they all know they need forgiveness, some just allow it to get lost."

"What can we do?" Jael asked.

"I can't tell you that, but I can tell you that you can't end it. You have to keep going. You have to figure out a way," she said.

Odella spent the remainder of the day discussing the options with the Princes. She did her best to convey how the Humans thought, how they could be so controlled by fear. Odella understood the Human mind. She had been a Human, she had been a great ruler. One who was appointed by the King himself. She had walked with the King in her human form. She understood the Human weaknesses. She knew firsthand about forgiveness. And more importantly, she knew the King and the Princes. With all that she had within her, she convinced them to continue on with The Plan.

Night came before they knew it. An attendant had lit the candelabras. Magnor had somehow forced himself to make his way to the table, but was very reserved. The tables had been cleaned, as best as the servants could clear them, and the night fare had been set out.

From down the corridor, the King turned the corner heading toward the Dining Room. He was not surprised to see the Queen sitting on a chair just outside the doors. As he approached, she put her finger to her lips signaling him to be quiet.

"How long have you been out here?" he asked.

"Most of the afternoon," she said.

"And no one has come out to find you?"

"No. Only the servants, and of course, dear Waldemar," she said.

The King reached down and took the Queen's hands in his. "Have you had dinner?" he said.

"Yes. Waldemar had it set up out here. He's such a dear; he keeps giving me updates as if I can't hear what's going on." They both laughed. "Shhhh," reminded the Queen. "And how are you?"

"This is not easy," answered the King.

"No it is not. We knew that from the beginning. They will make it, they may need to be pushed a few times, but they will succeed," assured the Queen. "Are you ready to go in?"

"I've not seen her yet," the King said.

"She's as beautiful as ever," the Queen said. "I'm sure this was not the way she had intended to make herself known."

"Do you think she ever had intended to do so?"

"She would have - eventually. Their love and bond is too strong. Neither would have been able to exist without seeing the other."

"Shall we go in?" the King asked.

"Yes, I guess it's time. But be prepared, Magnor has fainted once already today."

"NO!" said the King in disbelief.

"Shhhh! You have to be quiet," reminded the Queen once again.

An attendant opened the door and was startled by the presence of the King and Queen. Both put their fingers to their lips to prevent him from announcing their entrance. They quietly stood unnoticed, listening.

Odella sat engrossed by the discussion and along with the others in attendance, were unaware of the King and Queen's arrival. Waldemar was the first to make their presence know, "Good evening, Sir," he said.

Odella froze. She closed her eyes half hoping that this would all vanish but fully realizing that this wasn't a dream. Jael, once again, took hold of her hand. Odella opened her eyes and turned to see the silent guests. The room fell silent. As Magnor watched, he felt a part of him, the part that had been broken beyond repair, begin to stir. The anger and hurt was being pushed aside, as the desire to rescue her filled his being. He breathed in life and love and joy and forgiveness. They filled his entire being, forcing out all resentment and fear. She was beautiful. She was dirty. She was broken. She was Odella, and he loved her beyond his own understanding.

Odella and the King locked eyes. He smiled. Oh, she had not seen his smile for a lifetime. "Did you finally finish whatever it was that you were so tediously working on outside the window?" he asked. She was speechless. Tears flowed freely down her soft cheeks, but she couldn't help return his smile. Forgiveness filled her brokenness, and she felt herself being made whole.

"Not yet, Sir," she forced out.

"You will," he said. "You have plenty of time."

She knew she had to - she knew she had to address the Queen. How could she? How could she ever look into her eyes ever again. Jael, once again took her hand. She felt Jael's gentle guidance to stand and she did so. Odella stood motionless; tears flooded her eyes. Jael began to walk toward Mother and gently pulled Odella through her resistance. As she took a step forward, she found the strength to look up. Everything in the room vanished. All she could see was her Queen standing with open arms waiting to welcome her home. Odella could not stop herself. She dropped Jael's hand and ran into the Queen's arms.

"Welcome home, my dear. We've been waiting for you."

Chapter Nineteen

Since Odella's intervention, the Princes had dedicated every hour to coming up with a strategy. The Dining Room had gone through a clean sweep. Carasi and Ferrul had revisited all the tablets and notes; hesitant to toss them all, they sorted and filed them away. When the two realized the small stack of papers remaining were all that could be of any possible help, it was so pathetic, it was funny. The attendants were thrilled that it was no longer a challenge to find cleared places to set the platters and place settings. The dinner hour was approaching quickly. Only the attendants had come and gone; the Princes had not left the room.

"Is it simply that we have to find another Prophet?" Konnory asked exhausting all possibilities.

"I truly don't think that is our answer," Carasi replied. "They have a much shorter lifespan these days."

"Too true. Once a Prophet is recognized, Patho issues an all out attack," said Ferrul. Ferrul and Carasi now sat with two tablets in front of them, mostly filled with blank pages.

"We keep saying that! Is there not something that can be done to extend their life?" asked Konnory.

"I don't believe so. Patho seems to have perfected this particular attack," Carasi said. "Maybe we should make the Watchers visible?"

"You are joking, right? If Patho had any idea how many Watchers were in Turayn..." Ferrul replied.

"Well, we need more than a Prophet," Jael said.

"What do you mean?" asked Konnory. "A warrior?"

Magnor leapt to his feet. "Yes, let's send warriors and get this over with!"

"That's getting old, Magnor," Ferrul said with very little emotion. Ferrul began writing on a new page. "This is no longer a battle just against Patho, it has become a battle against most of the Humans on Turayn. We are also battling the Empire."

"The Empire?" Magnor asked.

"Yes, the Empire," Konnory answered. "The Human is his worst enemy. Who would even think to take Father's laws, which were intended to enhance their lives, and turn them into death sentences? This group claims to be speaking for the King, but they are far from it. They have created an entire government around Father's laws and uses force to control the rest of their species. I doubt Patho even knows it's happening. But I'd bet he's taking the credit for it."

Carasi stood up and walked over to the window. He saw Odella working in the garden once again. He recalled everything she had told them. He also remembered the stories Father had told about a young boy who killed a giant. He turned and said, "It may be time for one of us to go." The suggestion took everyone by surprise.

"What do you mean, go?" Konnory asked. "Like I went?"

"Yes," said Carasi, as he returned to the table.

Konnory stood and began to walk around the room. No one spoke. It was a suggestion that had crossed everyone's mind but no one had verbalized it. He wasn't sure if he was the best choice, or for that matter, if it would even do any good. But if that is what it was going to take, he was willing to do so. Despite things being much simpler and definitely less crowded when he was there, he still felt like he understood exactly what Odella had said about life in Turayn. After a lengthy silence, Konnory spoke up, "I suppose, I'd be willing to go back."

"No," said the King, as he entered the Dining Room. All eyes turned toward him expecting an explanation, but there wasn't one.

Jael stood and made his way to the fireplace. He was certain they were making the right decision to continue The Plan. He also believed he understood why Konnory couldn't go back.

J. G. Bruenning

This had been his idea from the beginning. Everything he had fought so passionately for was in jeopardy. He glanced at Quaine and Palti's empty chairs. They had been empty for far too long. He turned towards his Father and said, "I will go."

There was barely even the sound of breathing in the room for minutes. Ferrul looked at the King. "Father, do you have any objection?"

The King scanned the room. He stopped as he looked at each one of his sons. Lastly, he looked at the two empty chairs. "I have great concerns, but I do not believe there is any other option," replied the King. Little more was said, and the King left the room as quietly as he had entered.

The King and Queen did not join the Princes for dinner. The Dining Room was unusually quiet during the meal. No one seemed to be able to express exactly why this worried them all so greatly. Each one of them retired that evening with the heaviest hearts they had felt since the day of Patho's great deception.

The family was all present the following morning for breakfast. Although the room was filled with light, there was a heaviness that made it feel dark and dreary.

"I must get to my tasks," Mother said, as she excused herself from the table. "You all have a lot to talk about." The Queen walked to the far end of the table where the King sat. She put her hand on his shoulder and gave it a gentle rub. Looking at her attendant she asked, "Are you ready?" With a nod, the two made their exit.

It only took a few moments of silence for the discussion to begin. "He'll have to go as a child," stated Carasi.

Carasi looked at Ferrul. Ferrul was shocked at the thought. He then turned to Jael, "That does seem to be the only way possible. Would you be willing to do that?"

"That's extremely dangerous!" Magnor insisted. "Turayn has become so volatile. We can't send a child. It just isn't safe! Besides, how great of a difference could a child make? We need an adult."

"And where exactly are you planning on coming up with an empty adult human body for Jael to go into?" Konnory asked Magnor quite pointedly.

Jael looked at Father. There was something in his eyes that Jael had never noticed. "Father, do you think this is right? As long as you believe there is a chance it may work, I will go, regardless of what is required of me."

There was a new depth Jael felt as they locked eyes. "If there is a possibility to redeem all of this - this will be how." The room once again was still. They couldn't explain their uneasiness. The King took a sip from his cup. Folding the napkin that lay in his lap, he placed it next to his empty plate. He stood, and with a gentle nod, excused himself and quietly left the room.

"I so wish he would tell us what he is thinking," Konnory said as the doors closed. Again, the room was still.

After a few minutes, Carasi brought their attention back. "We will need to have control over his birth. We can't risk him being born to parents who won't understand. They'll probably even have to be warned beforehand."

"Exactly. We can't leave this up to a random choosing. It's not as if Jael has put in a request for redemption," Ferrul added. "This has to be two people that understand they are giving themselves over to the King.

"Who will we get? How will we choose them?" asked Magnor.

"For that, I believe we will have to rely on the Watchers. They will be able to guide us to our best options," Carasi replied.

Konnory sprang to his feet and bolted out the door. He descended the stairs in hopes to find Balbas on duty. He would know. He would be able to offer guidance. As he rounded the last landing, Balbas flew down past him. "Balbas!" Konnory cried out.

Balbas came to a sudden and complete stop. "I'm so sorry, Sir, I didn't know it was you."

"Is there somewhere you need to go?" Konnory asked.

"No." Balbas look at him expecting an explanation.

"You were in such a hurry, I just thought you were on a mission."

"I'm always on a mission. But never too busy for a Prince. Now, what can I do for you?"

"Can we sit down? This is a little complicated." Balbas lead Konnory to a table, and the two sat facing each other. Konnory glanced around the room, the Watchers and Messengers had not yet come into his focus. Balbas waited. It was only a few moments later that Balbas could tell that the busyness of the room was in Konnory's sight.

"Now, what is it that you need of me?" Balbas asked once again.

"We have decided it's time to strengthen our presence in Turayn."

"Is the King going to raise up new prophets?" Balbas asked with great excitement.

"Not exactly," answered Konnory.

"He's not planning a war, is he?"

"No, nothing like that. Magnor's the only one in favor of a war."

Balbas tilted his head and raised one brow, "Is Magnor going to start a war?"

"No. And if you ever hear such a rumor, you go to the King directly!" Konnory instructed. "We, the Princes, that is, have decided it's time for one of us to go."

"One of you to go?"

"Yes."

"Is the King aware of this?"

"Yes."

"And he agrees?"

"He has given us his approval."

"Interesting."

"How so?" Konnory asked. Balbas hesitated. "Balbas, why is this so interesting?"

"Oh...well..." he closed his eyes and looked up. He began tapping his fingers on the table, one after the other in succession. He started with the other hand. The beat grew faster and louder.

"Balbas?" Konnory said softly.

Instantly the percussion stopped. "I see!" Balbas said with a massive grin. "I get it! You need a way for him to enter Turayn unnoticed."

"Exactly." Konnory replied.

"And he's willing to do this?" Balbas asked.

"Yes."

"Jael is certain this is what he wants?"

"Yes, but how did you know it was Jael?" Konnory asked.

"Because, he is the one." Balbas was suddenly calm and relaxed. Konnory could feel his emotional change from across the table. "You will need two humans. We'll have names for you immediately."

"Balbas, how did you know?"

"He's been down here a lot," Balbas replied.

"Who, Jael?"

"No, the King. I've learned to watch and listen. The King isn't so hard to figure out if you simply watch and listen."

"He told you this was planned?"

"No. Well, not in so many words. But it makes sense now. What you've all decided is right." Balbas pushed his chair away from the table. "If there is nothing else, I have work to do."

"Thank you, Balbas. I'll be expecting names."

Balbas stood and left the table. Konnory watch as he engaged a small group of Watchers and Messengers in conversation. From time to time they all glanced over in his direction and then returned to their discussion. A short time later, they were off, and Balbas was engaged in a new conversation.

A Messenger was sent to ask the Watchers whom they thought may be the best options to become Jael's parents on Turayn. They had to be completely genuine in their commitment to the King and be fully dedicated to seeking forgiveness. They would need to be from an area with a high concentration of Humans seeking forgiveness. Most importantly, it was decided they needed to be people who were exceptional on the inside, but almost unnoticeable on the outside. There could be nothing that gave Jael away until he was ready, otherwise Patho would put an end to him immediately. After an extensive evaluation process, a couple was chosen.

Balbas organized it all. Watchers were sent to the Humans to request their assistance. Their willingness to accept such a request, as well as their understanding of its importance, would have been unmatched by anyone else. By accepting, these two people's lives would be changed forever. Their sacrifice would be great.

As the first Messenger was sent, Balbas gave strict orders to offer assurance and elevate any fear they may have. "They are Humans. Remember this," he had instructed. "They are fearful of everything and everyone. Patho has made sure of that.

Be prepared, they won't believe you. They need assurance. Speak softly. And don't appear suddenly or we'll lose them all together. Slow, gentle, and soft! Don't forget."

The Messengers did as expected, and with Balbas's flawless execution, Jael's transformation to Turayn was established.

Jael's appointed time was in sight. The King remained quiet and reserved. Those who were aware of this venture seemed solemn and uncertain of what was to come. Jael had decided that he would spend time alone in preparation for his entrance into Turayn. It would by no means be a normal entrance. Jael hadn't abandoned the Kingdom and therefore had no need for him to submit a request for forgiveness. He also wouldn't be born without a recollection of the Kingdom. He would spend the final time alone in the garden, which had been hidden from the inhabitants of Turayn.

As the family was finishing their dinner, Waldemar entered the Dining Room. "It's time," He said as he bowed to Jael. Jael made his way to each one of his brothers and said his goodbyes. Little else was said. Jael hesitated before approaching the Queen. How could he be apart from her? As he walked into her open arms, he was surprised at her strength. "You are the only one who can save this," she whispered. Jael did not want her to let go, but eventually she did. He turned and faced the King. The King embraced Jael as if he might refuse to let him go. With a kiss on each cheek, the King sent Jael on his way.

Jael made one last stop before leaving the Kingdom.

"What should I expect?" he asked.

"You can't expect anything." Odella removed her gloves and set them on the ground next to the flowers she was planting. "It's taken on a life of its own. The lives people lead and the problems they face are so different they almost don't make any sense here in the Kingdom. And unless they are one of the lucky few like the Prophets, their lives here before The Deception make equally as little sense to them. Don't expect anything, Jael. But watch them closely. Here in the Kingdom, what is inside someone is no different than what everyone sees on the outside. On Turayn, that is incredibly rare. There is an abundance of pain and fear that hides who they really are inside. I know that you will care enough to look for what is truly inside." With that, she embraced Jael and kissed good-bye.

Jael would be completely alone in the garden until his life on Turayn began. The Kingdom felt cold and empty with his absence. Waldemar built a warming fire in the Dining Room. This room was no longer a place of planning and strategizing; it was a place of gathering and comforting and waiting. Waldemar made sure the King's favorite drink and delicacies were always available; however, few were ever consumed.

"It should happen any moment," Ferrul said quietly. The King and the remaining four brothers were gathered around the fireplace. "Yes, we should receive word any moment."

At that exact moment, Tayten entered the room. "It's complete. He made it. Jael has successfully entered Turayn as a Human."

There was a huge collective sigh that seemed to breathe air back into the room.

To Abaddon,

The king has been quiet for some time now. It is time to make a move against all the Humans still seeking forgiveness. Report immediately on the current state of Turayn so I can devise the best course of action to permanently evict the king from the Human's minds.

Highest,

Patho

To our most brilliant strategist Patho,

There is really only one group remaining still devoted to the king: the Humans from the kingdom of Hadad. They are not exactly small in number, but their temple has already been destroyed once when they were conquered by another kingdom and forced to leave their land. Unfortunately, they were able to build a new one shortly afterwards when another kingdom conquered the first kingdom that had conquered their kingdom. Despite all of their struggles, most of them have refused to turn from the king.

Your servant,

Abaddon

Abaddon,

I realize that at times, intelligence is not your strongest asset, but I am not enjoying the pain in my head that your last report has caused. Our plan of attack is this:

1.Continue to inspire rulers in that area to war. If the king's pets can't be conquered, let's at least lower their numbers.
2.Get them to split into even smaller groups with different ideas and beliefs. It should be a simple task with that ludicrous list of laws the king gave them.
3.Eliminate any who stand in my way.

Your Highest,

Patho

Chapter Twenty

Jael's birth was a simple one. On the outskirts of the hustle and bustle of a busy town, Jael came forth as an infant. His human parents were of little means with other children to care for. His human mother watched over him with great expectation and an uneasy reluctance. She was young and innocent herself. Why was she chosen? What would the son the true King become? Even though he was an easy child to care for, it didn't mean that he was it still human, with human needs. His mother nursed and cared for him. She so wanted to tell the world who this infant was, but she had accepted the responsibility and she was determined to uphold her commitment.

As a small child, Jael loved spending time in his Human father's workshop. His father was a carpenter which meant most of his income came from doing odd jobs for people around town.

Unlike the Fallen Souls who arrived in Turayn, Jael had memory of the Kingdom. This was very difficult to make sense of for a Human infant. The King had assigned Watchers to surround Jael from the moment he entered Turayn. They were ordered not to make themselves known to him and to most certainly not speak to him until they were permitted to do so. No one was sure how the young Human Jael would respond if he was aware of the Watchers.

When Jael was only a few years old, he watched his Human father work passionately on a small chair. It was unlike anything else Jael had ever seen him make before. The detailed images carved into the wood triggered memories of the chairs that sat in front of the massive fireplace in the castle. He began to see glimpses of his brothers, not as Princes, but as children being read to while sitting by the fire. As Jael grew in human form, so did his memories.

Jael's parents attended Temple regularly. They offered sacrifice. The stories of Hadad, Ada and others were a part of Jael's life from the time he could talk. He attended Temple with his parents as often as he could. His mother marveled as she watched him. He seemed to understand much more than the teachers were actually saying.

As he matured, so did his questions, many times astounding the local teachers. He drew out ideas and details that they had never considered. As time passed, visits to the Temple became essential to him. On several occasions Jael's simple question would spark a debate amongst the leaders that would last long into the evening. Jael enjoyed observing the debates as much as he enjoyed contributing to them.

Jael's love for the Temple Teachings went deeper than his love for knowledge. These were stories of Humans he felt he knew personally. These were the records of the stories that he had heard Father tell at the dinner table. Hearing them allowed

Jael to relive the days of creation with his brothers. He held on to those memories, for now it was the only connection he had to the Kingdom.

Jael and his Human siblings were expected to help take care of each other and help provide for the family. Whether it was his sisters helping their mother make fabric, or the brothers helping them carry the fabric to the market to sell, or helping their father with his work, there was a lot to be done and they were always willing to help one another. They were also always willing to take time off when it was possible. He and his brothers spent most of their time by the water. Jael loved the sea. Fishing, swimming, or simply taking in the beauty, he never tired of it. He loved his brothers and sisters, but as his recollection of the Kingdom grew, his loneliness grew as well. Magnor, Ferrul, Carasi, and Konnory were such a part of his life. He longed to be sitting around the table with them.

Jael's Human father had returned to the Kingdom while he was still somewhat young. Death was something Jael had never experienced prior to his arrival on Turayn. He had seen quite a bit of it by the time his father passed. Death was no longer new to him. However, this was the first of someone dear to him. He and his human father had a very close bond. Jael had grown very aware of the sacrifice his father had made by accepting the responsibility to care for him. If it were not for his willingness, there was little hope that The Plan could succeed. Jael knew they would someday meet in the Kingdom. What a glorious day that would be. This anticipation made it a bit easier for Jael to handle. The pain of losing his Human father was so similar to the pain he had felt when Quaine and

Palti had left the Kingdom. The hope of their return home had borne Jael's determination to fight for The Plan. The thought of his Human father returning there now, and the wonderful celebration that was likely taking place that very moment, made Jael determined to see it through regardless of what it may require.

As Jael reached adulthood, he worked hard to make sure that his mother and siblings would be prepared for his leaving. By this time, he had full recollection of the Kingdom. He daily thought of Quaine and Palti. He was also aware of the distance between them. It had been over thirty Turayn years since he had any contact with the Kingdom. Jael struggled between the memories of the Kingdom and living in this world. There was no one in Turayn that could understand.

The Kingdom was aware of every detail of Jael's life in Turayn, and it was no easier for any of them to have been apart from Jael. Although time passed slower in the Kingdom, the time separated from Jael felt an eternity. The King and Magnor had a large room in the castle transformed into the communication center. The King was briefed continuously on the events of the day.

"Sire, the time is drawing close. Jael has been making arrangements to leave his home. We are at the threshold of the next phase," Waldemar said calmly.

The King clapped His hands in celebration. "Then, it is almost the time when I will be making visits to Turayn." There was great excitement in the King's voice.

"Yes, Sire, it is." Delight filled the eyes of the King. "Jael has a few more tasks to accomplish. By all appearances, he has made it this far without raising any suspicion from the Pit. That will likely change very shortly, and we expect Patho to approach this issue personally."

"Jael will be able to handle him, of this I am sure," assured the King.

"Now, let's discuss your visits," said Carasi. "We believe mornings are the best time. Jael wakes before the roosters and we know that the Pathonians don't tend to get moving until about midday. If your meetings are in the morning, and are never in the same place, it should go largely unnoticed by Patho."

The King sighed. "I could just seal them all in the Pit now and be done with this." They knew he was joking, yet at the same time very serious.

"That time will come," said Ferrul. "There's...let see here. There is just a short time left before you'll have your first visit. We are constructing a Viewing Tower to allow you to watch Jael's activities prior to your visit.

"Jael has been guided to the river?" asked the King.

"Not yet. The Watchers are to make themselves known to Jael shortly. They will instruct him to meet the Baptizer on the river bank," answered Konnory. "After that, things should begin to move very quickly."

"And we are certain the Baptizer will be there?" asked the King.

"Most definitely. The Messengers will make sure of that and have given us no indication that he will not follow their lead."

"Once we reach that point, we really have no way of knowing for certain what will happen," explained Ferrul. "It will all rely on Jael. There is no knowing how long it will be before Patho catches on, and we can only guess what action he will take. All are on alert. The armies have been training rigorously."

"They must be. Magnor has been there for some time." said the King.

"I believe it comes with the added bonus of allowing him to avoid Odella," the Queen added.

"Regardless, the troops will have benefitted from it by getting the extra attention. We hope for the best, but are ready for the worst. There are no guarantees." The King rose and thanked everyone for their service. Taking the Queen's hand, the two left the room.

When the Viewing Tower was complete, the King and Queen were escorted there accompanied by Waldemar. The anticipation was enormous. Uncertainty and expectation battled within each one. Jael was a Human now; there would be no semblance of his Kingdomly self.

As they approached the Viewing Tower, the King realized Ferrul and Carasi were already in place. Konnory was following close behind. Magnor stood at attention as the King reached the steps. He was in full uniform, and a hundred officers surrounded the Viewing Tower's base. The King was full of pride for his sons. Jael may be the one who is in Turayn, but each of his brothers was in full support and working every moment to ensure their brother's success.

As the King and Queen looked out from the Viewing Tower, the King recognized the land he was looking down on. He had walked those roads with so many. He knew the hills. He recalled his visits with Hadad, Lior, and Jair. He knew this kingdom, Turayn. He knew it very well.

They saw the mass of people by the river. The Baptizer was in the water speaking to a man. The King focused in on him. In an instant, the King realized that the man was indeed Jael. His emotions sent a huge charge of energy through the Kingdom. The figure was most definitely familiar, but it wasn't until he turned around and the King could see his eyes, that he knew it was his son. He wanted to shout out his name. He wanted to make his way to Turayn, to walk and talk with him. In that moment, more than anything, he wanted to bring him home.

As they looked on, they watched as the Baptizer took Jael in his arms and slowly lowered him into the water. The King knew that there was no longer any way to protect Jael while he was in Turayn. Jael had taken on this responsibility willingly, without reservation. As Jael was brought back out of the water, the King's emotions were more than he could contain. The words themselves weren't very loud when they left the King's mouth, but the emotion behind it amplified them and carried them to every corner of existence: "This is My son, in whom I AM well pleased!" No one moved, not even the King. When the vibrations calmed, the Queen reached over and took his hand. No one was sure if it was heard anywhere outside of the Kingdom.

Jael heard it loud and clear, and it was the most beautiful thing he heard since entering Turayn. How he had missed his Father's Voice. The Baptizer heard it and suddenly, deep inside, he remembered. He fell to his knees and wept. Those on the shore heard it and were sure they had just witnessed something great.

Quaine heard it and raised his head to the sky, "Father, oh Father, how I have missed your Voice."

Palti heard it. Palti wasn't sure where he was exactly. All he knew was that he was surrounded by a blinding darkness. The Voice sent shivers down his back. He wasn't sure how he felt; feelings were a thing of the past. It had been a long time since he had felt anything. The last thing he remembered feeling at all was anger.

Patho fell out of bed when he heard it. He didn't know what had just happened, but anything that woke him up, and especially something that could make him fall out of bed, couldn't be good. He began shouting out orders and directions in such a way that all of the warlords were tripping all over each other.

Patho stumbled his way out into the middle of the Pit, searching for answers. "Any word yet?!" he yelled at his secretary.

"Yes," the secretary began. "Apparently the Baptizer, the hairy guy by the sea who's been promising to wash away sins by dunking the Humans in the water..."

"Is he still doing that?" interrupted Patho. "I don't understand -- as if they think they can wash me away. The King tried that once, if I recall. I'm still here!"

"Anyway," annoyed by the interruption, "apparently he baptized someone this morning and when the fellow came up out of the water, the Voice was heard," continued the secretary.

"Does anyone know who the man was?" asked Patho.

"No," answered the secretary. "They say, he's headed to the desert."

Patho stormed out of the room, "Send word to Abaddon that I am on my way!"

Chapter Twenty-one

Jael rose early as he did every day. The Watchers had prepared him with instruction as to when and where he was to meet Father. This was the first time the King had visited Turayn since Jael's arrival there. Jael would venture out into the desert. As he had felt the need to spend time in the Garden prior to entering Turayn, he once again felt the need to have time alone. Time to prepare for what was ahead of him. The desert was just that place.

"Jael," the King called.

"Father," Jael sighed. He ran towards Father who stood with open arms. The two embraced, and for a moment, Jael forgot where he was.

"Tell me of the Kingdom," he said. He listened as Father offered greetings from his brothers and recounted recent events. Jael could see it all. For but a moment, he was home. He knew now why these visits had been so important to the King and even more important to those who walked with him.

Each morning the King and Jael met. It was a time of reflection, a time of instruction, a time of questioning and discovery.

"Have you met my *other father*?" Jael asked one morning.

"Yes, yes I have. A great man he is; such strength. He reminds me of you," the King replied.

"Really?" asked Jael.

"Yes. He may have been your father, but you were his teacher," said the King. "He is one of the few who loved his work in Turayn so much that he has requested to be further trained in woodcarving. I understand he has taken on quite a project."

"I can't wait to see it! And how is Mother?" Jael asked.

"She sends her love." said the King. The image of the Queen burned in Jael's memory, it was so real he could almost feel her.

"From the moment you entered Turayn there has been a group of Watchers protecting you. They have been by your side every moment of every day." Jael smiled in response. "You were aware?" the King asked.

"Not at first," Jael responded. "But as my memory and awareness grew, so did my awareness of my surroundings. As a child, there were moments I felt as if I saw someone, or something standing next to me, but when I turned my attention - they vanished. I ask my parents a few times, father only smiled and mother would say, 'You can never be sure.' Later on, there were times I was sure I had full glimpses of them. I knew they were always there. It's been a great comfort. I would get away and sit by the water, knowing that I was surrounded by those of the Kingdom. It's allowed me to feel as if I was home, if only for a few moments."

The visits with Father were wonderful. Except for the desolation of their surroundings, Jael could almost pretend he was home. But it couldn't last forever, he knew there was an appointed time to leave this place, and he knew he must return to his life among the Humans. He and Father would have other chances to meet, but their future visit would not be so long.

"Do you still believe there is hope, Father?" asked Jael on their final walk.

"I believe that there must always be hope," replied the King. "Are you regretting the decision you made?"

"Of course not, Father!" Jael exclaimed. "Even if there was no hope I would have made the same commitment. It's just that I can't picture what it will actually require to redeem Turayn. We planned for everything. We tried to foresee any move that Patho might make. He no doubt takes credit for the difficult lives the human live, but he actually had very little to do with it. The Fallen Souls are doing most of this to themselves. Dealing with death and disease and the natural things that come along in Turayn is difficult enough. The greed, jealousy and anger that is inside them, and the things they are capable of doing to each other because of those feelings...Patho may have been able to corrupt the

sacrifices, but the Fallen Souls are more of a threat to The Plan than he is now."

"None of them realized what it would mean for them when they left the Kingdom. Even for those who return, the guilt of having left is very difficult to overcome. They are not the same individuals we knew them to be before they left. Anyone is able to ask for forgiveness, but only those who actually seek it are able to find redemption," said the King.

"There is a world of difference between forgiveness and redemption."

"Indeed there is," said the King. "The danger the Humans pose to themselves and others is unavoidable. All of them are vulnerable to it. Even Odella, Waldemar, and Tayten had their moments. But despite their mistakes, they continued to seek forgiveness. In some ways, those weaknesses, the wicked thoughts and actions, are what allowed them to find redemption."

"I see that now," Jael said.

"Our time is coming to an end," Father offered.

"I wish it were not so," Jael replied.

"I am always close by," said the King. "You need not worry about your protection..." For a moment, Jael's eyes were opened, and he saw the Watchers that surrounded him.

"Father," began Jael.

"Yes, son," the King replied.

"What will it take?"

"It will be made clear to you. In due time, my son, in due time. Now I must leave. You have work to do."

Alone again, Jael began walking towards the nearest village with a heaviness that seemed to contradict his passion and dedication. He felt he had glimpses of what was needed to be done in order to save The Plan. Most of the time, however, it was like looking through the morning mist that hung over the water. He had been in Turayn for over thirty years already and the situation was as dire as ever. He was going to need some help.

"Jael! Is that you?" The call interrupted his thoughts. Jael continued walking. He had been expecting this. He knew Patho would find him eventually. It wasn't surprising that he would arrive just after Father returned home.

The voice got closer, "Jael, I knew that was you." Again, Jael didn't respond. Then, suddenly a figure appeared in front of him. "Didn't you hear me? Jael, what are you doing here?"

"Walking," Jael responded.

"I know you," pointing his finger toward Jael's face, "you're Jael."

"I may be, but you do not know me."

"No? Really? I would swear you're an old friend of mine from another place."

"We are not, nor will we ever be friends," Jael said directly.

"What are you doing away from the Kingdom?" Patho looked around at their surroundings, "and all the way out here?" Jael did not reply.

"Come, I want to show you something." Patho motioned for Jael to follow. Instantly, Jael found himself on the top of a mountain. As they stood looking at the vastness of Turayn, Patho continued, "Look at this amazing world. This can all be yours. I will happily hand it over to you. It only requires you to join me! You and I together could accomplish anything."

"This place is not yours to give," Jael responded.

"It IS mine! I OWN it! I control it ALL!" Patho shouted. He glared at Jael but found no reaction from him. He leaned his head to one side to relieve the tension building in neck. Jael noticed that Patho would close his eyes tightly and jerk his head about. Being in the vast Darkness had not done him any favors. Patho was a bundle of nerves, causing him to twitch and jerk. Patho did his best to appear that he had regained his composure, "And it can be yours as well."

Jael stood motionless. The silence made Patho's involuntary motions increase. "It is not yours." Patho spun around. Jael was so bold and confident in his speech, he had thought that the King had spoken. "It will never be yours!" Patho's nostrils flared. "Leave me!" Jael commanded as he looked Patho directly in the eye -- a gesture Patho could not tolerate. With a sigh of disgust, Patho turned and vanished.

As Jael stood, gazing across Turayn, he knew that everything had changed. He was under Patho's detection and there was no doubt Patho would be watching. Going forward, there was only one guarantee; Patho could attack at any time.

Jael would need people around him as often as possible, people he could depend on, people he could trust. People he could teach, and people who could help him reach as many Humans as possible in the time remaining.

A few hundred yards away, a tree crashed to the ground. It was too far away from him to have been a real threat, but close enough that he was certain to have noticed it. He suddenly noticed something else; he could clearly see the Watchers. Father wasn't exactly correct when he called them a group; there was a multitude of them. A much larger group than Jael had expected.

Jael stood for a moment in awe. They were magnificent and yet fierce. Jael saw very little difference between them and the

Warriors who stood guard around Turayn. He also saw that there were several of them standing between him and the fallen tree. Jael turned his attention back to the village ahead of him and laughed loudly as he began walking.

Abaddon,

I have located Jael. He has fled the kingdom on his own. It is difficult to tell whether he is merely jumping ship before it sinks or if he intends to claim Turayn as his own. I do not intend on handing it over to him. Undoubtedly, he will realize the power I have over the Humans and join our cause soon. The king will know that not even the sons that remained by his side are safe from me.

Your Highest,

To our ruler and prince-stealer Patho,

We will keep a close eye on Jael and keep you up-to-date on his activities. He cannot be foolish enough to think that he could fight you for Turayn and win. If he does, he will surely suffer the consequences.

Your servant,

Abaddon

Chapter Twenty-two

During the next weeks, Jael petitioned the Watchers to look for people who could assist him. Acting on Odella's advice, Jael decided to find worthy followers by determining who would accept his call freely, without convincing on his behalf. As he stood on the shore, he saw a small group of fisherman in the distance. He watched as they threw their nets out in great hopes of a good catch. With each cast, he heard their disappointment as they retrieved empty nets from the water.

"Throw your nets on the other side," he shouted out.

"Won't help," one called back.

"Give it a chance," he shouted. He heard their mumblings and could tell he had stirred a debate amongst them. He watched as eventually two of the men did as he suggested. As the nets hit the water, he heard the ridicule of the others in the boat. Within moments, the ridiculing stopped as shouts for help began to echo across the water.

"Help us! There's too many to bring in."

"We're going to break the nets!"

"Get over here and help!"

Jael smiled as the small boat was overtaken by lively, flapping fish. The men fought to keep the fish in the boat. He waited as they struggled to row themselves and their overloaded vessel to shore.

Once safely on dry ground, the two brothers who had taken his suggestion walked over to him. "Who are you?" one of them asked.

"We had been out there all morning, how did you know were the fish were?" asked the other.

Jael put his arm out and rested his hand on the shoulder of one. "You are brothers, I assume?" The two nodded. "I have a task for you, are you willing to join me?" They looked at each other and for some unexplainable reason felt that if they passed this up, they would regret it forever.

"We will," they spoke in unison. Without looking back, they walked along the shore and away from their fellow fishermen.

Jael loved the sea more than any other place in Turayn and spent as much time there as possible. His morning discussion with the fisherman had made him a familiar face to many. The first four of Jael's followers were all fishermen who put their nets down on the ground at Jael's first invitation and dedicated themselves to following him. They were two sets of brothers: Gad and Micah, Thad and John.

As was his practice from a small child, Jael entered the Temple each Sabbath. It was common for him to sit amongst the Rabbi's in debate. This day when opportunity presented itself, he stood and began teaching. He quickly gained the attention of everyone. They had not heard teaching like this. They heard the familiar stories from the Temple Writings, but this man spoke of them as if he had been there. He talked as though he knew each character personally. He taught with complete certainty and without any of the lengthy, confusing explanations they were used to from the teachers.

As the morning passed, the crowd continued to grow until the Temple was filled to capacity. It was a crowd the Temple Leaders could not remember ever in attendance. As each newcomer entered the place, they were instantly engulfed in silence except for a gentle lone voice coming from the center of the audience.

A man entered who did not follow the reverence of the others. He pushed his way through the crowd, shoving aside anyone who stood in his path. He was small in stature but his great determination made him forceful in his attempt. He caused a great disturbance. By the time he was face to face with Jael, his presence was undeniable. Standing inches away from Jael, he began to address him in a voice that vibrated through the Temple.

"Jael, why have you come? Are you here to get rid of us? We know you son of the King!" The magnitude of his voice and forced way of speaking did not mirror the physical size of the intruder. The sound of it sent chills through the audience. It was not like any Human voice they had ever heard.

"Be quiet!" Jael commanded. Gasps were heard across the room. With great authority Jael continued, "Leave this man. Go!" The crowd fell silent once again as the man began to tremble. He fell to the ground. Jael's newly appointed followers instantly took steps toward the man to assist, but he held out his hand to stop them. Jael watched closely, as did the Watchers who had also infiltrated the room.

The crowd witnessed as the man seized on the floor. It was only Jael and the Watchers who were able to see the Pathonian leave his body. From the severity of the man's struggle, they knew he had been inhabited by this undesirable guest for some time. Instantly, the man fell into a state of calm and lay at Jael's feet. Jael motioned for his four followers to assist the man, and they jumped into action. All were aware of what had just happened, but they were unable to make sense of it.

After the great commotion had ended and the man had been escorted out surrounded by two of the Jael's followers, Jael motioned to the Watchers to assist. This newly freed man would need extra protection as Patho did not handle loss very well, even the loss of one Fallen Soul.

As Jael was leaving the Temple that day, a large figure who was the complete opposite of the earlier intruder, brushed up against him. Jael turned. Standing in front of him was the Baptizer. "My friend, I had hoped to see you again," Jael said, as he held out his hand in greeting.

The Baptizer grasped Jael's arm. He scanned the crowd. Jael saw the awareness in his eyes. "I fear I don't have much time left, but I wanted to speak with you," said the Baptizer.

"Of course." The two men stood in the midst of a constant flow of people but as they locked eyes, all the commotion vanished. In an instant, the rest of the world vanished as well. "What do you need of me?"

The Baptizer leaned in closer. "I know who you are," he said tightening his grip on Jael's arm. "You are the Son of the King. I knew you the moment I saw your eyes. When I heard your Father's voice," Jael heard the crack in his voice. "the rest of me awakened. Whatever the good is that you are here to do, the seeds have been planted. Many are desperate for forgiveness, but many are still being led astray. You are our only hope, Jael. May the King be with you." With that, he embraced Jael as he would a lost brother, turned and disappeared into the crowd.

Jael's four newly appointed followers recognized the Baptizer and stood in amazement as the two conversed. Was this a normal day in Jael's life? Were these the types of events they would be witnessing if they continued to follow him? It was a question they all had in their minds but were not yet comfortable enough to express. Jael took note of the questioning in their glance.

"I believe we have an appointment," Jael said addressing Gad and Micah. "Why don't you lead the way?" The two lead Jael to their home. Conversation was limited as they walked through the streets. It wasn't for a lack of questions, each could barely contain the private conversations in their heads, but being new on the job, none left led to verbalize them.

As they entered a small but inviting home, they were informed that the lady of the house had fallen ill. Gad and Micah rushed in and found their mother lying sick in bed. Jael followed the two into the small dark room. He walked over and stood by the side of her bed. Reaching his hand down, he took her hand in his and said ever so gently, "Come, your sons are here to see you."

Gad reached out his hand in an attempt to stop Jael, but Micah quickly stopped him. The four men watched as the sickness instantly left her. Color returned to her face and slow deep breaths replaced the shallow rapid breathing of moments earlier. She sat up with Jael's assistance. Sitting on the edge of the bed, she looked up at him and then to her sons. Her smile came from the depths of her soul and calmed any doubt they may have had about their decision to follow this one. She rose to her feet and left the room.

Pathonians, the Baptizer, Teacher and now Healer; the brothers had witnessed amazing things already. An excitement began to grow with each of them. Something told them they had only begun to see what this new life they had chosen was going to be.

Word spread quickly about the events of the day. The retelling of the healing caught on like a wild fire and soon all of the village's sick were gathered around the home. Jael would not have refused any of them had it not quickly become dark. As Jael and the brothers talked late into the night, they received word that the Baptizer had been arrested and beheaded.

Early the next morning, before anyone else had risen, Jael met the King. He could sense the heaviness in his son's heart. "Father, I was not expecting this."

"What part?" questioned the King.

"How is anyone able to change things when Patho and the rulers here are so quick to end lives, especially if they view those lives as a threat to their power?" he asked. "How much time can I possibly have to do any good? Crowds have already started to gather around me."

"There is no way to tell, my son. You were wise to seek out people to surround yourself with, and you will continue to add to their numbers. They will provide you extra protection, but more importantly they will allow you to reach out to more." The King hesitated. "But you know as well as I that you will always be under attack as long as Patho knows you are here."

"I just hope I can do what is required in the time that I am allowed. The Baptizer had only been at the river for a short time, and now his time is no more."

The King said nothing for a few moments. "Death is a very powerful thing, and it may yet cause a great deal of good, if that person was determined to do great good."

Chapter Twenty-three

Crowds had begun to follow Jael everywhere he went. It became commonplace for his followers to be sitting around a room in someone's home sharing the Temple Writings, while crowds of strangers surrounded the exterior in hopes of catching a glimpse or hearing a word from Jael. On this particular afternoon, the home was filled to capacity. The home itself was surrounded by those who couldn't enter. These listeners were at times three and four persons deep.

As Jael spoke, he heard a commotion above him. Mumbling spread across the group. He looked up toward the roof to see rays of daylight beginning to break through. He continued watching, and in a short time there was a large hole. The roof commotion increased, and then through the hole, a mat began to be lowered down. He heard the voices of those above calling out direction, "Gently, lower him gently."

A moment later, a mat lay on the floor at Jael's feet containing the rigid body of a young man. Jael looked up to find peering down through the hole four heads staring back.

"What would you have me do?" Jael asked them.

"We believe you can make him walk again," one replied.

Jael looked at the thin weak young man lying before him and from above, his four friends. Images of his brothers filled his memory. He smiled. Jael reached down to meet the outstretched hand of the skeleton form. "Get up and walk," he said. "May your faith be as great as that of your friends."

It was as if all in attendance could visibly see sickness rise from his body and life consume it. Cheers began to ring out from above. The young man released Jael's hand and rolled off the mat. Life radiated out from him and filled all who were watching. He stood before them examining himself. He moved his fingers, flexed his arms, patted his stomach and ever so slowly began moving his feet. They worked! He bent his knees and the frail joints popped and cracked as newness began flowing through them. And then he began to dance. The crowd parted to provide him space to move. Jael watched in delight. Nothing thrilled him more then watching Humans being set free. The expressions of celebration filled the room but it did not drown out the noise from above. There were four on the roof -- who were celebrating too.

Jael was constantly aware of the great needs around him. Everywhere he went, he was asked to perform great acts of the Kingdom, a term his followers used to describe the miracles they observed. Jael did not separate himself from daily life in Turayn, instead he chose to participate in every aspect of it.

On one occasion, his Human mother had invited him to attend a large wedding celebration with her. Without hesitation, Jael accepted. During the event, the host ran short of wine. Jael's mother rarely asked Jael for assistance, so on this evening when she approached him and inquired if there was anything he could do, he obliged. After agreeing, she turned to the servants of the host and directed, "Do whatever he tells you." The command made Jael chuckle. He loved this woman. She seemed so unnoticeable from the outside, but he knew her strength firsthand. He also knew the sacrifice she had made for him. He would do anything to provide for her.

Jael turned jugs of water into wine that night. It wasn't any type of wine that Turayn had to offer. It was far beyond what the Humans could produce. Jael enjoyed it more than anyone. Standing under the evening sky, he sipped it slowly. Gazing up into the heavens, he was reminded of his last words with Mother. He was beginning to understand that there was more to all of this than just being the one to come to Turayn. Closing his eyes he took another sip. It was a taste of the Kingdom.

The Temple leaders questioned everything Jael said and did. He used the same Temple Writings they did, but he didn't focus on the rules, instead he spoke of the King's provision. It troubled the leaders greatly, but mostly it threatened them. During a visit to the Temple, he was once again approached by a man asking for healing. Jael did so and told the man to not tell anyone what had happened. Of course, the healed man was unable to keep the news quiet; he began speaking of it as soon as he walked away.

The Temple leaders approached Jael: "How can you do these things on the Sabbath? Do you not know that is our day of rest?" they insisted.

Upon hearing these words, Jael recalled the day the King had set the seventh day apart, making it a day of rest, a day of joy. Even this had been distorted. The Sabbath was no longer a day to reflect the goodness of the King. Instead, it had become a day filled with lists of rules, of all the activities that were not allowed to be performed on this day. There was even a list of things that could cause you to end up in prison.

They are unaware that enforcing all the rules was as much work as - work, Jael thought to himself. Jael drew his attention back to those questioning his actions.

"Was man made to serve the Sabbath, or was the Sabbath made to serve man?" Jael responded. No one answered. "How is it that you have missed so much? You are only concerned about rules and you use those rules solely as a way to judge the unworthiness of others. Have you not read of Hadad?" This type of rebuke, which they were not accustomed to receiving, further angered the Temple leaders. They had no response.

Since Jael's baptism, his demeanor had changed. He may have once been thought of a man of few words, but no longer. On the contrary, those who heard him speak would immediately tell others of what they had heard. At times, Jael found himself surrounded by hundreds, perhaps thousands. He used this time to tell stories as a way to explain the Kingdom and the love of the King.

"There was a farmer," Jael began, "who desired to have a great harvest. This farmer selected the best seed. He toiled the soil, removing anything that may hinder the growth of his crop. He carefully planted the seed. With great care and delight, the farmer tended to his crop. At harvest time, additional help was required in order to bring in the harvest. The farmer prepared a great celebration for his friends, neighbors, and those that assisted in the harvest. During the celebration, the farmer was told that this great harvest was fortunate.

"'Fortunate?' replied the farmer, 'this has nothing to do with being fortunate! I chose the best seed. I made sure the ground was prepared. I took great care in planting each seed. I tended to the crop each day. Even with all that effort, it was because the King provided the sun and rain to make it grow. It is because of the King that we benefit from a great harvest.'"

Jael loved to speak about forgiveness. "A very wealthy man had three sons," he began. "Each son worked closely with the father and tended to all his business. Then one day, the middle son approached the father and told him of his desire to leave and make a name for himself. He requested his inheritance. The father reluctantly fulfilled his son's request.

"It did not take long for the son to waste his inheritance. He was left with nothing. The only work he could find was shoveling manure from the horse stables. One afternoon, covered with manure, he realized that being a servant in his father's house would be far better than his current situation, and the middle son began his journey home.

"As he drew closer to his father's home, he saw a figure in the distance. He realized it was his father running to meet him. The father received his son with open arms. He ordered new clothes to be brought. He sent word that a celebration was to begin in honor of his son who had found his way home.

"When the older brother returned that evening, he heard the noise from a distance. 'What is happening in my father's house? It sounds like a celebration?' the oldest son inquired.

"'Your younger brother has made his way home, and your father has prepared a celebration,' replied a servant.

"This angered the oldest brother. He was filled with great jealousy. The oldest brother set out to find his youngest brother in hopes of convincing him to address this unjust forgiveness. The oldest brother searched and searched, but was unable to find the youngest.

"The father came out of the house to find his oldest son. 'What are you doing out here?' he asked. 'Why are you not inside celebrating with your brothers?'

"'Brothers?' the eldest questioned.

"'Yes. Your brother has returned home, and your youngest brother and I are in the house celebrating. Please come join us.' Anger overtook him and the eldest son was unable to join in the celebration. In fact, he never entered the house again. There are those that will choose not to enter the Kingdom."

As Jael finished teaching, a man approached him. The man was dirty and unkempt; his body was covered with bruises and scars. He was a man of great strength. Around his wrists and ankles were the remnants of chains that once confined him. He stood calmly in front of Jael. His breaths were deep and sporadic. His muscles involuntarily jerked. Jael looked at him and through his eyes, could see his soul. He gently said, "Come out of him!"

The man fell paralyzed at Jael's feet. "What will you do with us? Please do not torture us!" His followers watched. The voice was audible but the man's mouth did not move. The questioning came from deep within shouting out to Jael.

"What is your name?" Jael asked.

"We are the Multitude," the voice echoed. "Please send us back to the Darkness, free us from Patho's control. Send us into that herd of pigs." Multitude did not demand the request from Jael, for he knew to whom he was speaking. Multitude, who had inhabited this man for some time was not made up of Patho's followers. Rather they were thousands of Others. Patho had assumed control of them when he found them in the Darkness. They were taken by force. At one time, they had joined together and requested their freedom from Patho's service. Outraged, Patho bound them together and sentenced them to possess one human soul for the rest of eternity. They had lost count as to how many human bodies they had inhabited. As each human had grown weak and unable to endure their presence, Patho would confine them to a new body.

Jael looked around and saw the large herd of swine Multitude had requested. The pigs numbered into the thousands.

"As you request," Jael said. "Leave this man and find your rest in the pigs." The man's body began to seize violently as Multitude left him. Jael witnessed the increase number of Watchers who surrounded him. Once out of the man's body, the Watchers surrounded Multitude and escorted them to the hillside. Jael watched as the spirits entered into the pigs. Instantly, the pigs became out of control and fled down the hill into the waters below. Jael's followers watched in fear and amazement. As the last pigs were consumed by the water, the Multitude was finally free from Patho's sentence.

Jael helped the man to his feet. Gad and Micah took him to the shore and aided in washing him and tending to his wounds. Thad and John found clothes for him to wear.

When they presented him back to Jael, he was a new person. Calm, gentle, and confident. The man pleaded to be allowed to accompany Jael and serve him in any way possible.

"No," said Jael. "You must go back to your village and tell your friends and family of your freedom." With tears flowing down his face, the man embraced Jael and ran toward home.

Sometime later, the King and Queen were gathered with the Princes in the Dining Room when the door opened. There stood the two commanders who oversaw the processing of the requests from the Fallen Souls who still remain in the Darkness. "Sire, we have received a request and are uncertain how to direct it. This has been the first request of its kind," they said, as they stood before the King.

"What makes it so unique?" asked the King.

"It doesn't appear to be from a Fallen Soul, rather it is signed by 'The Multitude'," replied the senior of the two commanders. "We've done some research, and it appears to be one or several of the Others."

"The Others?" Ferrul asked.

"Who left the Kingdom prior to Patho?" Carasi finished.

"Correct," nodded the officer.

The King turned and looked questioningly at Ferrul and Carasi. The two brothers looked at each other for a moment before returning their gaze towards the King.

"It should work," said Ferrul shrugging, with only the slightest sense of uncertainty.

To our lone worthy potentate, Patho,

Jael continues to be closely watched. He spends the major-
ity of his time with a handful of followers, but there have
been reports of large groups gathering to hear him speak. He
is already creating enemies with some of the local religious
leaders over the laws. We are focusing on uncovering his
agenda.

I am pleased to report that the Baptizer has quite literally lost
his head and poses no further threat. As it turns out, he wasn't
as hairy as we thought; he was wearing furs as clothing. I don't
think that had anything to do with the smell, however.

Your servant,

Abaddon,

Excellent. It is safe to say that Jael cannot be trusted. Take any steps necessary to distort his message and cause as much conflict as possible between the local leaders and his group. Make sure the leaders learn of anything Jael does that goes against their version of the laws. Implant enough fear and suspicion in their minds that they begin to see him as nothing but a threat.

Get the Empire involved. They can put pressure on the Temple to further your efforts.

Your Highest,

Patho

Abaddon,

Have you received any reports on Multitude? From my calculations, it's time to assign them into a new Human. You know how much I enjoy watching this ritual. Nothing is more satisfying than observing a Human lose total control. My hunger is deep. Send word of their location.

Your Highest,

Patho

To the highest among all, Patho,

The search has begun to locate Multitude. They won't be difficult to find. All we need to do is follow the path of their destruction. It was ingenious to cram so many of them into one being. In the meantime, may I offer up a few good-doers to satisfy your hunger?

We've recently discovered SHAME. It's a very useful tool. Keeps the guilty focused on themselves. And you know that self-obsessed humans are easy to consume.

Your servant,

Abaddon,

Shame!How relentless. This will be of great use especially to those seeking forgiveness. Keep them focused on themselves. This could be the very thing that voids anything the King is offering.

You may have quenched my thirst, but my hunger increases.

Your Highest,

Patho

Chapter Twenty-four

The number continued to grow of those who had accepted Jael's call and became his close followers. The Watchers had selected both men and women who had been diligent in seeking forgiveness. When Jael approached them, they instantly accepted his invitation and were eager to follow and serve him. It was a very diverse group and Jael loved their differences. It was the differences in his own brothers that he loved the most. However, he had never experienced this measure of diversity. Men and woman working side by side; learning, growing and serving.

On this particular afternoon, Jael was deeply engrossed in conversation with his followers. They frustrated him at times, but for all their faults and inability to understand most truths, he loved them dearly. As they discussed the rules that were handed down through the generations, a knock came to the door. Gad answered it; Jael could hear the conversation from where he was seated. As Gad led the man into the room, Jael rose to greet him.

"My daughter is sick, I am afraid she will die. Please, I beg you, come," the man said. Jael recognized this man. He had seen him many times in the Temple. This man asking for his assistance was the Overseer of all the Temple Leaders, a group that did not embrace Jael or his teachings.

"Do you truly believe I am able to heal her?" Jael asked.

"Yes, I do," the man replied, as he bowed his head in honor. Looking up he said, "And I also believe that if I doubt, you are able to help me believe."

Putting his hand on the man's shoulder Jael assured, "Then we should go!" Jael gathered his things and made his way out the door. By this time, stories of the acts of the Kingdom had spread throughout the land. Each time he stepped out of doors, he was engulfed by people needing his assistance.

Accompanied by his followers, they pushed their way through the crowd. They instinctively encircled him in hopes to protect him, but today there were so many fighting for his attention that the mob was winning control. Then suddenly Jael abruptly stopped. The group that was following began bumping into each other as they came to an unexpected standstill.

"Who touched me?" Jael quietly asked.

"What do you mean, 'who touched you?'" replied Gad as the crowd continued to adjust their pace. "There could have been countless who did."

"No. Someone intentionally touched me." Jael turned around. The crowd had slowed, and as he turned, they began to step away as if Jael's words parted them. As they stepped aside, a figure was revealed. Kneeling in the dirt was a woman, head down and weeping. For a moment, the crowd had vanished and the only ones who remained were Jael and the woman.

With her head low to the ground, she confessed, "I did, Sir."

Jael reached down and offered his hand to her. She slowly raised her head and looked up at him. "I have been sick for years; no one has been able to help me. I have spent every ounce of energy and money on a cure. Everything I once owned is now gone. I have become a poor wretch confined to my home." Jael wiped her tears.

"I heard of your power. I believed that if I could only touch your robe, I would be made whole again." Jael helped her to her feet. She was weak and having difficulty balancing. She bowed her head again and continued, "I know I have broken many rules by coming to you. If the Temple Leaders knew that I was out in public...with this disease... they would..." The man who Jael was accompany by cleared his throat. The woman glanced over to him. Recognizing who he was, she was too fearful to finish and bowed her head in silence.

Jael put his hand under her chin and raised her head once again. "Yes, you have broken quite a few rules by coming to me. But there are times when breaking rules is what is required." Jael smiled again. "Did you hope I could heal you?"

The woman gently shook her head, "No, Sir, I did not hope - I knew - you could. I only needed to touch just the hem or even just a thread of your garment," she replied.

"Have you been healed?" he asked.

Tears flooded her eyes and once again began to flow down her dusty cheeks. "Yes! I have! I knew it the moment it happened," she said with great confidence. She took a deep cleansing breath. Jael watched as a smile began to break through.

"So did I." He stood strong as he steadied her. She stood for a moment lost in the gentleness of his expression. "Go," he said.

She hesitated, not wanting to leave. When she finally found the courage to turn around, the crowd came back into her sight. As she turned, she became a new woman. She took the first step, and the crowd that had stopped to watch took a collective step back. The group separated as if royalty was passing. She had arrived unnoticed in the crowd; she was leaving with every eye on her.

Jael watched. With each step, he could sense her strength returning, her stride becoming more confident, and her presence radiating from her. He turned and out of the corner of his eye, he saw another man running toward him. Upon his approach he turned to the Temple Leader. "Don't bother him anymore. She is dead, life left her a short time ago. There is no need for him to come."

Before the grief-stricken father could say a word, Jael reached out and grabbed his arm. "Don't be afraid," Jael said. "Only believe."

Jael motioned for the others to follow and they hurried to the man's home. As they walked, hope and despair flooded this father's heart. What can he possibly do now, he thought. They arrived to a home filled with friends and relatives overcome with grief. When they saw Jael, their grief quickly turned to anger and they began to accuse and ridicule that he was too late.

Jael wasted no time listening to their rant. He pointed to the door and addressing his followers commanded, "Get them all out of here." His followers sprang into action. Jael motioned for the man and his wife and they enter the girl's room.

The room was lifeless and cold. Lying on the bed was a small weak frame. Her skin was white and lips colorless. Her mother, being comforted by her husband began to cry. Jael looked at her with great compassion. "She only sleeps," he reassured. Turning back to the child he walked to her side and reached out his hand saying, "Wake up daughter." As those in the room looked on, the young girl awoke from her sleep. Breath filled her lungs, blood began flowing through her veins and color returned to her.

Before anyone could react, Jael turned to her mother and suggested, "I believe she is hungry, why don't you fix her something to eat."

With that simple request, Jael stepped toward the door when he felt a hand on his arm. He turned mid step. "Thank you," the father said softly.

Jael motioned for the others to follow, and they hurried to the man's home. As they walked, hope and despair flooded this father's heart. What can he possibly do now? he thought. They arrived to a home filled with friends and relatives overcome with grief. When they saw Jael, their grief quickly turned to anger, and they began to accuse and ridicule that he was too late.

Jael wasted no time listening to their rant. He pointed to the door and addressing his followers commanded, "Get them all out of here." His followers sprang into action. Jael motioned for the man and his wife, and they enter the girl's room.

The room was lifeless and cold. Lying on the bed was a small weak frame. Her skin was white and lips colorless. Her mother, being comforted by her husband began to cry. Jael looked at her with great compassion. "She only sleeps," he reassured. Turning back to the child, he walked to her side and reached out his hand saying, "Wake up daughter." As those in the room looked on, the young girl awoke from her sleep. Breath filled her lungs, blood began flowing through her veins, and color returned to her.

Before anyone could react, Jael turned to her mother and suggested, "I believe she is hungry, why don't you fix her something to eat."

With that simple request, Jael stepped toward the door, when he felt a hand on his arm. He turned mid step. "Thank you," the father said softly.

"We believe you can make him walk again," one replied.

Jael looked at the thin weak young man lying before him and from above, his four friends. Images of his brothers filled his memory. He smiled. Jael reached down to meet the outstretched hand of the skeleton form. "Get up and walk," he said. "May your faith be as great as that of your friends."

It was as if all in attendance could visibly see sickness rise from his body and life consume it. Cheers began to ring out from above. The young man released Jael's hand and rolled off the mat. Life radiated out from him and filled all who were watching. He stood before them examining himself. He moved his fingers, flexed his arms, patted his stomach and ever so slowly began moving his feet. They worked! He bent his knees and the frail joints popped and cracked as newness began flowing through them. And then he began to dance. The crowd parted to provide him space to move. Jael watched in delight. Nothing thrilled him more then watching Humans being set free. The expressions of celebration filled the room but it did not drown out the noise from above. There were four on the roof -- who were celebrating too.

Jael was constantly aware of the great needs around him. Everywhere he went, he was asked to perform great acts of the Kingdom, a term his followers used to describe the miracles they observed. Jael did not separate himself from daily life in Turayn, instead he chose to participate in every aspect of it.

On one occasion, his Human mother had invited him to attend a large wedding celebration with her. Without hesitation, Jael

Chapter Twenty-three

Crowds had begun to follow Jael everywhere he went. It became commonplace for his followers to be sitting around a room in someone's home sharing the Temple Writings, while crowds of strangers surrounded the exterior in hopes of catching a glimpse or hearing a word from Jael. On this particular afternoon, the home was filled to capacity. The home itself was surrounded by those who couldn't enter. These listeners were at times three and four persons deep.

As Jael spoke, he heard a commotion above him. Mumbling spread across the group. He looked up toward the roof to see rays of daylight beginning to break through. He continued watching, and in a short time there was a large hole. The roof commotion increased, and then through the hole, a mat began to be lowered down. He heard the voices of those above calling out direction, "Gently, lower him gently."

A moment later, a mat lay on the floor at Jael's feet containing the rigid body of a young man. Jael looked up to find peering down through the hole four heads staring back.

"What would you have me do?" Jael asked them.

Jael smiled, "Only believe," he gently replied and continued through the door. Accompanied by his followers, he made his way to the seaside.

Early the next morning, Jael walked the shoreline with the King.

"Father, there are so few who have faith. They have replaced their belief with rules and rituals." Jael began.

"I know," said the King.

"Did not Waldemar live by faith and not rules? Did he not make sacrifices to you daily out of faith? Hadad had rules, yet he entered each battle by faith, faith that you would be with him. When did those actions lose their meaning?"

"This is the greatest flaw of the Human soul. Humans don't allow themselves to trust their emotions. They are driven to create rules as a way to be in control."

"The leaders don't use the rules to control their emotions, they use them to control their position and keep everyone else beneath them."

"I know, my son," said the King.

"They use every rule as a tool to judge others. Everything they have done is an act of passing unfair judgment or finding ways to judge them more. They are unable to enjoy any part of this life. It is beyond my understanding," said Jael.

"They become so obsessed with trying to follow the rules that they can't focus on anything else. Everything they do is self-centered, and the leaders and rulers are not exempt from this. They do good things only because of what they believe they will gain by doing so. They are filled with guilt at the same time they are celebrating an achievement. The Human is consumed with - the Human," said the King.

"We will never be able to change their way of thinking. It has become so imbedded within them - I don't know what it will take," said Jael.

The King looked at him for a moment and then continued walking. "You'll find a way," he said softly.

Jael paused and looked questioningly at Father. "This is larger than any of us were aware, isn't it?" Jael finally asked.

"Yes, Jael, it is." They walked on.

Chapter Twenty-five

O ne day shortly after his morning walk with the King, Jael was approached by a few fishermen who were asking about forgiveness. As he began to answer their questions, a small group who was also passing by joined them. As the morning hours grew, so did the crowd. In a very short time, there was assembled on the hillside a very large group eager to hear every word. Toward evening, Jael realized that his large audience had been sitting and listening most of the day. There was no doubt they had grown hungry. Turning to his close followers, he asked, "What shall we give them to eat? We must feed them."

"How?" replied Gad. "We don't have the means to feed them. What do you suggest we use?"

"That is what I'm asking you," Jael said very patiently but directly.

"There is no place that could sell us the amount of food it would take to feed this crowd!" Benjamin said.

Jael looked back at the crowd that covered the hillside. "Have them sit down," Jael instructed.

"And do what?" Gad asked also looking across the crowd. He was calculating just how many were in attendance.

"Where is your faith? Do you still not believe after all you have seen?" Jael shook his head in disbelief. "Let's start with what we have."

The discussion went back and forth for a bit until Thad approached the group with a small bundle in his hands. "There is a young boy here with some bread and a few fish that his mother sent with him for his own lunch. He has offered it to you." Thad held up the small lunch in his hand.

"Leave it to a child!" Jael said as he receive the food. "We shall always start with what we have." Jael raised his head and looked into the sky saying, "Father, thank you for your provision." Jael began to divide the bread and handed it to his followers. As the followers made their way through the crowd, each was amazed that their portion never ended. In fact, after all had been served, there was plenty leftover. Thousands were fed that day. After all had eaten, the crowd began to disperse and returned to their villages. Jael instructed his followers to return home as well. Then entered a boat and began the journey back without him.

Jael sat alone on the hillside. He recalled the recent conversation he had with the King. He remembered the day he and his brothers sat around the table discussing the possibility of The Plan. How Father seemed so distant, so aloof. He recalled the day the King stopped the planning process and instructed them that he, and he alone, would be responsible for what was to happen next. They were not to speak of it but only trust his wisdom.

He thought of the recent events. The woman who broke all the rules because she knew, not merely hoped, that he could heal her. The father who asked for his daughter to be healed, because he believed, and understood that even if he doubted there was faith for him. The boy who willingly gave his lunch. These compared to the Temple Leaders who only talked of rules and rituals.

"What will it take?" Jael asked himself over and over.

In the distance, Jael could see the boat his followers were in. A wind had picked up and they were struggling to keep the boat on course. *Even these men,* he thought, *these who have seen firsthand what faith can do, cannot manage to hold on to it for any length of time.* He watched a while longer as they struggled to keep the boat in the proper direction. Jael stood, taking a deep breath, he began to walk out onto the water.

As the frightened crew caught glimpses of a figure walking towards them, their imaginations got the best of them, and they became consumed with fear. Panic erupted within each, and they thought they were being taken over by a spirit. Jael walked until he stood a few yards from the boat. When they realized who he was, Gad immediately threw his legs over the side and sat on the edge. The others yelled for him to get back in the boat, but he was determined. The wind and wave circles Jael, but he stood steadfast on the surface of the water. The sea splashed up against the boat rocking it from side to side.

Gad heard the cry of the other crew members. He look down and saw the water, the endless bottom. He looked out and saw Jael. Keeping his eyes on Jael, Gad pushed himself off the edge and stood upright holding tightly to the boat, feeling its support. The others gasped in the realization that he was not sinking. With his eyes firmly focused on Jael, Gad released the boat. He took a step and then another. The wind hurled, the water splashed; he took another and then another.

Those in the ship were speechless. Some too terrified to speak, others wishing they had his courage. With the next step, Gad looked down and was consumed with the realization of his situation. The next thing he remembered was Jael's hand reaching down and pulling him up out of the water.

The crew helped Gad back in the vessel. Jael turned to the sea and commanded its stillness. Instantly, the wind died and waves softened as Jael entered the boat. He so wanted to keep walking by himself, but he knew these men needed him. Jael entered the boat and continued the journey with them.

"Why? Why?" Gad asked. "Why couldn't I do it?"

"But you did," Jael responded. "You were doing it. I knew you could."

"But I went under," Gad said still gasping for air.

"You took your eyes off of me and onto the storm," Jael said. "You focused on the situation not on the possibilities."

The crew began bailing out water and reorganizing the deck. Gad sat quietly with his head down. Jael moved to the front of the boat and settled in.

"Why were you so afraid?" Jael asked once everyone had calmed down.

"We thought you were a ghost," answered one of them.

Jael had to stop himself from laughing, "After everything you have seen, is it still easier for you to believe that a ghost is walking in the middle of the sea than to trust me?" They arrived safely to the other side under the clear night sky.

The following day, Jael was eating with his followers in the marketplace. The Temple leaders approached them, and they questioned him about the way his followers were eating their lunch. There had been rules made about what and how to eat. The Temple Leaders felt that Jael and those at his table were not following the rules properly.

"It is not what you put into your body that separates you from the King, rather it is the thoughts and actions that come out of you," Jael said. Once again perplexed by his answer and unable to reply, the leaders left him.

"What did you mean?" asked Micah.

"Are you unable to open your minds? How is it that you have seen so much and yet your understanding is so small? Nothing you eat keeps you separated from the true King. For what you eat only affects your physical body. It is what is within your heart that keeps you separated. The King warned Bar's brother of this before he took his brother's life. It is recorded in the Temple Writings. You have heard it told since you were children. Each of you has the power within yourself to change. Separation comes from within. It is born in the heart and matures in your thoughts. You have to make the choice to allow it to control your actions. Separation is a result of your choices." Those in attendance were contemplating Jael's words for the remainder of the meal. Jael ate in silence.

Jael once again spent that night alone on the shore. As morning dawned, the King made Himself known. He sensed a difference in Jael's conversation; there was a seriousness and frustration that had not been there before.

"Father, they don't understand," Jael began.

"Yes, son, I know."

"Every time I start to believe they have grasped an idea, it's as if they never heard the truth," said Jael.

"In a way, they are blind. The blindness is not in their eyes. It is their hearts that are closed," said the King. "Fear plays such an enormous part in it all."

"Fear?" asked Jael.

"From the beginning, Patho has put all his effort into assuring that the Human is continually attacked by fear. It becomes imbedded deep within and most don't realize the control it has. It factors into their decision making. It stops them from being able to trust themselves and others."

"Then its fear that prevents them from having faith?" asked Jael.

"Yes. They no longer believe in forgiveness, instead they think they have to work for it, to earn it somehow. Fear tells them they will never measure up," said the King.

"Sacrifice used to be evidence of their belief in forgiveness, now it only shows their belief in the rules. For most there is no connection between the sacrifices and redemption," Jael said. "But The Plan requires sacrifice!" The King and Jael continued walking for a moment in silence.

"Father, there was a time in our planning that you stopped the process and said you would only know what happened next. This is what you saw, isn't it?" Jael asked. "This is the great sacrifice you referred to." The King nodded. "But Father, there are so many, so many who are still lost. I know I have only been here for a short time and at times I am angered by their inability to understand." Jael paused, "I love them so," he whispered. "I love them as you love me. I would do anything that will allow them to understand your love and grace."

"Anything, Jael?" the King asked.

"Yes, Father. Anything." They walked on.

Jael thought back to the day before Patho's rebellion. There was a great sense of uneasiness throughout the Kingdom as whispers of Patho's mission began to circulate. The Princes had gathered with the King in the Throne Room; all of them except Palti. The King was calm and continued to reassure his sons that everything would be dealt with in a timely manner. Jael was the only one of the brothers to see Palti before he left.

Jael stopped and looked at the King, "Father, why did Palti leave?"

"He was angry," replied the King. Jael had never before spoken to him with such confidence and authority.

"Angry? Why? He's the eldest; he is next in line. The throne is his birthright," Jael said.

The King did not respond quickly. "When Patho became restless...I knew what lay ahead." The King hesitated. "Palti was not the one to make it right." The King paused, he selected each word carefully. "When I told Palti he wouldn't be the one to stop Patho, it angered him greatly." Jael could see the pain in his eyes. "When Patho left, Palti took the opportunity to make his exit."

Palti had been storming down the hallway the night before Patho's departure, Jael recalled. He had almost knocked Jael over as he came around a corner. There was no apology, he just continued down the hallway and yelled back, "Stay out of my way, Oh Great Offering!!"

Jael stood silent for as long as the scene had played in his memory, "Father, I am not worthy to fulfill such a sacrifice."

Chapter Twenty-six

J ael had few supporters among the Temple Leaders. The newly established Empire, whose sole purpose was to control the actions and behaviors of the humans, hated him as well. He was a threat in every way. Crowds would gather instantly when he started speaking. Although he used the Temple Writings, his interpretation spoke of freedom, love, and forgiveness; unlike the rules, rituals, and fear that they desired to instill.

Jael's popularity drew the attention of the Empire who pressured the Temple Leaders to keep him under control, a task they seemed unable to achieve. The Leaders were continually trying to find ways to stop Jael. They had become so angered by him that they wanted him to disappear. In an attempt to trick Jael, a group of them brought a young woman to him in a courtyard, claiming they had caught her in the act of adultery.

"Hmmm," Jael said. "Which one of you caught her?" he asked looking directly at the group. No one replied. Jael was not in a hurry to address them any further. He knelt down near the entrance to the courtyard and began writing in the dirt. After a long pause, he stood and spoke, "Stoning her is what the rule says...I agree. Anyone who stands before me who has not committed any wrong may throw the first stone." Jael knelt down again and returned to writing in the dirt. He turned his back to the group as not to witness what came next.

The men fell silent. Jael heard a few of the stones hit the ground as they dropped from the accusers hands. It was the eldest leader that moved first, but rather then moving toward the woman, he slowly began making his way toward the gate to leave the courtyard altogether. He was quickly followed by others. As each one left, they saw what Jael had written, a single name; Hadad.

It took little time for the courtyard to empty, and all that remained was Jael and the woman. Jael walked over and taking his outer robe covered her. He raised her head with his hands and wiped her tears. He attempted to look directly into her eyes, but she would not meet his.

"I make no accusations against you. Go, you are forgiven. Remember your freedom." He wrapped his robe around her tightly and it covered her completely. He caught her glance as she turned away. He saw her pain. In his mind flashed images of Odella wandering in the Darkness. The day she burst through the doors. The first time she looked at Magnor. He felt his heart break. He was determined to do anything and everything within his power to offer life to these who were so damaged. To those who had yet to find their way home. As a tear escaped his eye, Jael turned and walked away.

That evening, he and his close followers shared their dinner. Jael asked, "When people ask you who I am, how do you respond?"

"You are the great teacher!" Gad said confidently.

"The great healer!" Thad added.

"But who do you believe that I am?" Jael was looking directly at Gad.

"You are the Son of the King!" Gad said boldly.

For the first time, Jael began to tell his followers of The Plan. He told them details that he himself had just recently began to realized. His followers listened intensely. Some with great understanding, others became overwhelmed by such details. It was apparent that Gad was greatly disturbed by the information. Unable to contain himself, he jumped to his feet and shouted, "That will never happen! We will never allow it!"

Jael heard Carasi in his voice. He was taken back to those early discussions of The Plan. At first, The Plan was about protecting the Kingdom and Father's throne. It had a new focus for Jael. He had seen firsthand the consequences of being separated from Father. The emptiness of living a life in fear. He knew his Father's heart; he saw the potential that these Humans could have if they would only allow the King to be a part of their lives. The Plan was about forgiveness. Forgiveness opens the door into the King's presence. Jael knew there was nothing his

Father would not or could not do for those who choose to walk through that door.

Jael looked at each one individually. These men and women he had shared so much with, who were once friends, brothers, and sisters in the Kingdom. These who had followed Patho and had turned their backs on the King. These who at times angered him so, whom he loved and was willing to sacrifice himself.

It was at that moment Jael understood the extent of the great sacrifice Father spoke. Mother's words echoed through his head, "You are the only one." It would cost him everything. Was he willing to lose it all for these? He was! With a determination greater than he had ever known, Jael turned to Gad and said, "Gad, where is your understanding? If you are not with me, you are against me. You are speaking Patho's words and I will not tolerate it!" The group was taken aback. Jael had shown his frustration in the past, but this was different. This was said with a new intensity.

The group watched in silence as Jael excused himself and left. He headed directly to the seaside. He spent the night contemplating these new realizations. Some overwhelmed him. He could understand Gad's anger. He couldn't get the image of the prostitute out of his mind. As morning approached, the King met Jael on the hillside. They walked for awhile without speaking.

"It has been made clear to me, Father."

"The road ahead of you is not an easy one," the King said reassuringly.

"No, Father, it is not. I don't pretend that it is."

They walked on without a word. The King was well aware that Jael had realized the extent of his mission here in Turayn. There was little more left to say. Jael held the power to stop the process at any time. The King had made sure of that from the very beginning. He trusted Jael completely. The next few days would be the darkest days either of them would ever face.

"Father," Jael began.

"What is it son?" the King asked.

"You saw all of this before Patho left." The King nodded. "Who else knew?"

The King was silent. As the gentlest smile emerged, he said, "There is nothing that your Mother is not aware."

Jael closed his eyes and stood motionless. He had admired their relationship. He thought he knew of her strength. He had never realized before that she and the King were one.

Jael turned and continued on. The King was right at his side.

"Is it clear what you will do next?" asked the King.

"Yes. I need one of the men to arrange for me to be arrested," Jael began.

"Do you know who you can entrust that to?" the King asked.

"I do. But it is such a great task, I'm not sure if he will agree. I'm not sure any of them would agree."

Chapter Twenty-seven

The capital was always very crowded during the week of the Freedom Celebration. This was a celebration that Father created generations ago when he freed his people from Egypt. Jael loved this time of the year. "What a great celebration!" he would say. "We must do this back home." He said it every year, yet no one was sure what he was talking about.

Jael and his followers were staying just outside the city. As the group walked to and from the city each day, Jael made sure he pulled each aside to spend time with them. There were things he wanted to tell them. He knew they would be on their own shortly, but he wasn't sure they were completely prepared for what was just ahead. Even though they frustrated him at times, he loved each of them. The next few days would be difficult. He wanted to reassure them of his love.

From the very beginning, Jael had watched Timar closely. He was an odd fellow, the oddest of the bunch to be honest. There were times he felt Timar could have possibly been a great warrior. He was stable, direct; he held himself and others accountable at a level that was almost unattainable. This caused friction between he and the others.

As the group walked back from the city to their dwelling, Jael walked alongside Timar. He intentionally walked slower forcing Timar's pace. The distance between them and the others grew. If it would have been possible to do so without drawing too much attention, he would have transported the two of them to the top of the mountain for this discussion. But such an act was out of the question. It would cause much commotion and would most likely draw attention from Patho. It may have been unfavorable to the one being transported.

"Timar, thank you for being with me," Jael began.

"Of course, I would not be anywhere else."

"We have done a lot of good here but there is much more to do," Jael said. They walked a bit in silence, the gap between them and the group growing. "Things are about to change. There is a plan in place that my Father has designed and that plan is coming to completion," Jael said, as he slowed their pace a bit more.

"You mean your heavenly Father?" questioned Timar.

"Yes?" Jael hesitated. He never thought of Father as heavenly. He was a King and kings are not heavenly. They continued walking. "A plan had been designed which offers forgiveness to any Fallen Soul who seeks it."

"This is the plan you spoke of the other day," Timar said.

"Yes, it is," Jael replied.

"May I ask, aside from seeking forgiveness and returning to the Kingdom, what part are we to play in this plan?" Timar asked pointedly. Jael was completely surprised. He had put off this conversation for nearly two days now trying to find the best way to bring it up, and Timar had just opened the door to the entire discussion.

"You all are to teach and remind. Teach people about the meaning of forgiveness and the true act of sacrifice. Remind them of who they truly are and where they came from and where they belong," Jael said. That was the complete answer in its simplest form, but it said nothing of the difficulty of the task.

"And how long do you expect we'll get away with that before we find our fates determined by either the Temple or the Empire?" Timar asked.

Jael knew now more than ever how true Timar's point was. "For some, I'm certain it will be much sooner than others."

Timar grasped Jael's shoulders and turned him so that they were face to face. "And how much sooner do you expect your time will come before all of ours?" There was no hesitation in his voice.

"I...how...," Jael paused for a second to collect his thoughts and his breath. "That isn't fully up to me to control."

"Sacrifice has always been the only way to find forgiveness and redemption. Now only a handful of those who continue to make the sacrifices find any salvation through it. How can we possibly redeem sacrifice at this point?" Timar questioned, desperately longing to find hope in Jael's answer.

"Sacrifice has become a ritual. They don't understand that the outward act of offering a sacrifice is just a representation of the inner sacrifice that they must make to return home. Sacrifice is not done out of faith, for most it is done out of obedience to the rules," Jael said.

"But how can we possibly change that without angering the Temple Leaders and possibly even the entire Empire?" Timar responded.

"By offering it for those who seek forgiveness."

"Surely you can't mean that we are to offer sacrifices for every single Fallen Soul who has found themselves born in this place?" said Timar.

They continued walking a short distance before Jael answered. "No. Just a sacrifice. One sacrifice to cover everyone. It will then be in the acceptance of, faith in and commitment to that single sacrifice that the Fallen Souls will find their way home to the Kingdom."

"What would possible qualify for such a sacrifice? What would be sufficient enough to allow every Fallen Soul that level of forgiveness?" Timar questioned with great intensity. They walked on. He replayed in his mind Jael's words hoping to find the answer. He recalled the day on the hillside when Jael said, "We will always use what we have."

He stopped. Images of the Kingdom flashed through his memory. Grabbing Jael by the arm, he spun him around. "NO!" he shouted. "I won't allow it! You are not simply talking of a sacrifice; you are talking about a separation from Father."

Jael was stunned. He was speechless.

"You won't survive." Timar was now inches away from Jael's face. His eyes were filled with anger and fear.

"I will, Timar. I will!" assured Jael.

"NO – you won't! I've been separated from him since that dreadful day. You won't survive!" shouted Timar ,as he raised his arms into the air.

"Timar, do you remember that day?" Jael questioned.

"Jael from that moment, that horrible moment that I stepped out of the Kingdom..." Timar fell to the ground. Jael immediately kneeled next to him.

"I will. I will survive. I will make it. I have to!" Jael said softly.

Timar raised his head, "No, Jael, it doesn't work like that. It's not that easy." Timar gasped for air. "It's horrifying! Words can't possibly describe the loneliness, the dread, the shame, the ache of being in the Darkness."

"It's our only hope, it's the only way. Forgiveness requires sacrifice. I am the sacrifice."

"NO!" he screamed leaving him once again breathless. "There must be another way!" Timar grabbed hold of Jael's robe and began pleading. "Jael, I've been there. I won't be responsible for you going there. You don't know what it is like to be separated from Father."

The words echoed though the stillness of the night. Jael didn't move. *Separated from Father? Who was he? There were only two who were separated from Father.* Jael felt his heart stop for a moment and then it began to race. No, it couldn't be.

Timar was now humped over, he groaned as if in great anguish. It was the sound Jael had heard fathers make as they stood over their dead or dying child. *The Darkness?* Jael's mind was racing and yet he couldn't think. His heart beat so loudly it echoed in his ears. He laid his hand on Timar's back. "Quaine?" he whispered. Timar sank into the ground. *Could it be? Had he found Quaine?* He had felt a connection with Timar, but he had never, even for one moment, thought that he could be the one he had come to save.

The two remained; Timar now almost lifeless on the ground and Jael huddled over him. Finally, lifting Timar's shoulders up, Jael raised his head with his hands. He had seen something in Timar's eyes, now he understood. Jael could do nothing more than stare into his face. For the last few years, these two brothers had been in each other's company without realizing it. Jael replayed all their encounters - trying to make sense of it, trying to understand why he did not know.

He then thought back to those early days when The Plan was being discussed. Quaine was the reason he fought so hard to convince the others to create such a plan. Quaine was the reason he had come in the first place.

"Quaine, don't you see, you are the reason I am doing this! It was your request; your pleading for redemption. I do this for you and because of you. I have ached for you since that dreadful day. I have hated Patho for deceiving you so. I chose - and I chose freely to be the sacrifice." Jael paused, "I will go to the end of the Pit for you. There is nothing you can say to change my mind."

"I am not worth it!" Quaine said.

Jael was quiet, deep in thought. "It's no longer only for you, my brother. I have seen... I have now experienced... the pain and suffering...you may have brought me here, but they are the ones for whom I give my life. I love them so. I love them as much as Father loves us."

These two brothers fell into each other's arms and wept. Their weeping washed away the hatred and anger toward Patho. It washed away any doubt of The Plan. Quaine had been found.

They spent all night together. Jael went back to the beginning of The Plan and laid out the details for Quaine. He told him of the days of creation, of Magnor's crazy designs. He told him of Konnory's willingness to be the first Human. He told him stories of Father's visits and how Waldemar, Tayten and Odella had returned. He told him of the book that recorded the names of the redeemed.

Most importantly, Jael told him of the events to come. He needed Timar's assistance. It would not be easy, but it was essential for The Plan to survive.

"I need you to turn me over to the authorities. I must be arrested," Jael said.

"How do you expect that will happen?" Quaine asked not fully understanding the scope of Jael's request.

"They are eager to end my life..." he said.

"Wait!" Quaine demanded. "You are going to willingly hand yourself over?"

"Yes. But they must think they have made the capture."

"I don't think I'm clear..."

"I need someone to hand me over to them in a way that makes them feel they are the victors."

"What do you expect will happen next?" Quaine asked with great hesitation.

"That will be in their control," Jael answered.

Quaine sat quietly next to his brother. He kept rolling his hands together and wiping the sweat on his robes. How could he say no? How could he agree? They had just found each other, how could their time be coming to an end? "I'm sorry Jael, I don't think I can do this."

"You can my brother. I need you to be able to do this. I know it's a daunting task, but I trust you completely. I had planned to ask you before I knew who you were. I trusted you then, I trust you even more now. That is the reason that I ask you to do it. It is the final act. We must trust Father. He saw this long before Patho ever left. We cannot quit now."

"But..., you..., I can't..."

Jael reached out and took Quaine's hand. "You fought for this. You risked it all in the Darkness to get word to Father. You initiated this," Jael said.

"But I am the reason you are doing this," Quaine argued.

"No, my brother, you are not," Jael assured. "This was The Plan long before either of us ever knew we needed one. We've both been working toward this moment for most of our lives. We can't turn back."

Quaine took a deep breath. This would be the hardest thing he had ever done. This would be worse than leaving the Kingdom. He could not bare the thought of it.

"Stop thinking," Jael said. "Trust Father." Quine squeezed Jael's hand. "We will survive."

When morning came, they were still talking, arm in arm. Jael was scheduled to meet Father. He thought about bringing Quaine along, but that might be too much for both of them. If Father had bellowed his proud remark on the day of his baptism, what would he do if he saw these two brothers side by side? He now knew that they would all be together soon. There was no longer any need to wonder where Quaine was, he was on his way back home.

"We must part. Tonight we celebrate. It will be the final time we are all together as Humans. You know what you must do. Everything depends on this. We do this together. You survived and I will as well. Father is close by and there is an army whose discipline and training has never been matched. I hold the authority to stop this at any time. We will survive." Jael took a deep breath and forced himself to let go of Quaine and walked away.

That evening, most of Jael's close followers were already in place for the celebration. Jael arrived with John. Timar was the last to enter. The meal began as usual. As part of the celebration, Jael gave thanks for the bread and divided it as he had done countless times before. As the evening progressed, Jael could feel Quaine's tension. As their eyes met, Jael nodded and Quaine stood, walked over to him and gave him a kiss. Each spoke the other's true names. As Quaine turned to leave, Jael grabbed his arm. Quaine hesitated but eventually turned back around. "I'll see you in the Kingdom," Jael said softly. Quaine stiffened; he patted Jael's hand and took his leave.

"...see you in the Kingdom," Quaine thought as he walked through the empty streets. Any other time, this would have been a great comfort, but tonight it was only a reminder of what would have to transpire for that to happen. He couldn't turn back. He was determined to fulfill his commitment to Jael. Quaine walked toward the Temple.

After dinner was complete, Jael made his way to a garden. It would be the last time he would speak with Father until he was in his presence. He wept that night; not because of the physical torture that was sure to lie ahead, but because of Quaine's words. Jael had refused to allow himself to think of the time that he would be separated from Father. It would not compare to the time he had spent here in Turayn. This separation had been tolerable. Being sent to the Pit, sent into the Darkness, having his soul separated from Father's was overwhelming.

"Do you want to end it?" Father asked.

Jael knew very well that if he said yes, it would take moments and he would be free. Patho would be bound to the Pit, and Turayn would be taken over by warriors. He also knew that there would be no more hope for the Fallen Souls who had not yet found forgiveness. Quaine would be saved, but he was no longer Jael's purpose. "No, Father. I will fulfill my commitment. I have allowed myself, perhaps for the first time, to truly realize that you and I will be separated, separated in an unimaginable way."

The King had never turned his back on anyone. It had always been the Free Will of those who left him that caused the separation. When Jael and the King would finally be separated, it would be an equal act of each: Jael in choosing to be the sacrifice, and the King allowing his son to do so.

Shortly after the King had left, Jael heard footsteps approaching. Quaine was leading a group of guards and Temple leaders into the garden. "There he is." With a kiss on each cheek, Quaine allowed Jael to be taken by the guards.

The King and Princes were receiving constant updates. They were not allowed to view from the Tower in fear of their reaction. As Waldemar informed them of this final act, he said, "With a kiss, Quaine handed Jael over."

"What?" insisted Ferrul.

"What do you mean, Quaine?" asked Carasi.

Waldemar hesitated. He had not intended to tell the Princes of his suspicion of who Timar was. "I'm sorry, so very sorry." He stopped searching for words. "As I've been watching Timar," he paused again. "It just seems to me that he is Quaine." The Princes looked at each other and finally to the King. Could this be? Could Waldemar be correct?

The King made no reaction, which was all the verification that Magnor needed. His chair fell backwards to the floor as Magnor stood up. "I'm bringing him home!" He was through the door and halfway down the hall before anyone could say anything. Then the mumbling began.

"Quaine?"

"He can't..."

"What will..."

"Quaine?"

"Magnor, you can't..." Eventually they were all focused on the King.

The King sat back in his chair. He glanced out of the window and then back to those sitting around the table. Ferrul jumped up and was heading toward the door. "Ferrul, let him go!" commanded the King. "It's all right. He is acting kingly, and there are times a king must do what he feels in his heart."

Magnor made his way to the stables and prepared his chariot. As he climbed on board, he noticed Konnory racing after him. He wasn't going to let anyone stop him, but to his surprise Konnory leapt up, grabbed the reins and thrust them into Magnor's hands. "I'm not missing this!" Konnory said. Magnor threw his head back and shouted. He gave his horses the command and they were off.

"What are you going to do?" asked Konnory.

"I'm not sure what WE are going to do," he responded. "We can't do what Father did with Lior."

"No, that won't do," said Konnory.

As they entered Turayn, Magnor drove the chariot to an open field where he could see a figure kneeling next to a tree. "There he is." As the figure made his way toward the edge of the field, Magnor saw a line of trees.

"You're not..." Konnory said. He rubbed his shoulder and sighed, "Just make sure you do it right this time."

"Have no doubt!" Magnor reached for his sword, and as they passed the trees, he leveled them with one fell swoop. With one last pass over the field, they saw Timar's empty body lying under the limbs. "Let's go welcome him home!"

To Abaddon and all who serve me,

The celebration begins shortly! Jael will be dealt with quickly and will soon be out of Turayn and in my possession for all of eternity!

Your Highest,

Chapter Twenty-eight

B y dawn the next day, Jael had been arrested, tried, and sentenced to death. He suffered terribly at the hands of the guards charged with watching over him. From what seemed like an eternity away, the King and Princes suffered through the details they heard during every update. The last report had left them with an image of a barely recognizable Jael heading towards the hill where his sentence was to be carried out.

The King refused to allow the Queen to be in the room. She had known every detail, every fear, and every possible danger since the conception of The Plan. She had supported the King in every decision. He wanted to protect her as much as he could by sparing her the horrific details. The Queen was in her chambers, and Tayten was given the responsibility of delivering her updates. It didn't really matter what kind words Tayten used, the Queen knew the reality of what Jael was experiencing.

The Dining Room was silent except for the information that came every few minutes and the sounds of footsteps, as

Magnor paced back and forth or as one of the others decided to stand elsewhere.

Heading down the hallway towards the Dining Room, Waldemar halted as he saw a figure dart into a dark storage room a few yards in front of him. He hesitated for a moment and then slowly walked to the open doorway of the storage room.

"The guilt comes from the part of us we can never get back," Waldemar said into the dark room. He leaned against the wall. "There's an innocence that comes from knowing that you have never abandoned or turned your back on your family and your King. Who would have known that asking for forgiveness would be so much easier than accepting it?"

"I can't...not yet," a voice in the room responded. "All of this is my doing."

The pain that had been inflicted on Jael's Human body was nothing compared to what he was beginning to feel now. He felt as though his actual soul was being stripped away as his last moments on Turayn began to fade. He was beginning to feel the separation and it was excruciating. With the last bit of life he had left, Jael cried out, "Father! Father! Where have you gone?" All of existence heard the crack of the King's heart breaking.

Patho had been waiting eagerly and leapt for joy as his two least untrusted followers, Serpent and Abaddon, led a quiet and broken Jael into the room.

"And to think, you could have had everything there! I offered to share it with you, and now I've got you here. What made you think that you could take everything from me? I can certainly understand why you would want to leave the Kingdom, I mean, the Prison. But thinking that you could just walk in here and take my territory was about as foolish as one can get." The smell of pride coming off of Patho was so thick you could gag on it. But Jael said nothing as Abaddon and Serpent sat him in the cell that Patho had specially constructed.

Patho turned to the two henchmen; he was confused by the expressions on their face. Instead of the triumphant look he expected, Abaddon seemed worried and uncomfortable. The uncomfortable part didn't bother him. "What could possibly be wrong with you two right now, at the moment of our greatest achievement yet?"

Abaddon spoke first, "Sire, I think we've been unaware of the true purpose of Turayn. It was never intended to be for the King."

"Well, I had figured that much out. But Jael is here, imprisoned! He's not going anywhere. Turayn is completely mine now!" Patho said, as he giddily jumped up and down.

"It wasn't for Jael either," interrupted Serpent. "It was for the Fallen Souls," he said coldly.

Patho stopped jumping, "The Fallen Souls are all lost. We made sure of that. What do the Humans have to do with them? There's no connection."

"The King has been offering redemption," Abaddon said with great hesitation.

"No. You mean the King is offering forgiveness. Of that, I was well aware," Patho insisted.

"I'm sorry, Your Highest, but it's not only forgiveness. He has been offering redemption."

"He's WHAT?!" exclaimed Patho as a chalice went flying across the room.

Abaddon dove under the nearest table, leaving Serpent to explain the rest. "The Humans are the Fallen Souls who have requested forgiveness. If they continue looking for forgiveness as one of them, they get to return to the Kingdom."

"And those who don't?" asked Patho.

"They get sent into the Darkness - forever," answered Serpent with a laugh.

Patho was stunned, "And you know this how?"

The answer came from underneath the table, "Jael's stooge, the one who betrayed him, explained it to the Temple Leader."

"And this has been going on..."

"Since - the - Garden," finished Serpent.

"OUT!!" shrieked Patho.

Abaddon dove out the door. Serpent took all the time he desired. Patho slammed the door behind them. They waited outside the room for hours listening to Patho's tantrum. Abaddon appeared ready to flee the moment he heard any sign of Patho nearing the door. Serpent, on the other hand, seemed to be enjoying himself immensely, occasionally laughing as he heard large items smashing to the floor.

Then there was an unexpected moment of silence. Abaddon leapt to his feet as Patho opened the door. He seemed to have calmed down considerably. "I've thought it over, and have come to the conclusion that this may not be such bad news. If this is true, then Jael is trapped here for the rest of eternity! I would gladly trade a few thousand of those idiots to have him expelled from the Kingdom forever. This is an even greater victory than I believed at first!"

As Abaddon and Serpent glanced inside the room, they noticed that despite the great deal of destruction Patho had caused during his outburst, Jael had not moved an inch.

Odella had left her work in the garden the moment she had heard the Separation between Jael and the King. She made her way into the castle. Not sure what her next move would be, she just knew she needed to be there. At first, she found it a bit strange to see Waldemar speaking into the storage closet. As she got closer, she heard what he was saying. She placed her hand on Waldemar's shoulder as she stepped past him and entered the darkened room. She reached down and helped Quaine to his feet. She led him out into the hallway. His face was soaked with tears as both Odella and Waldemar embraced him.

A short distance away, inside the Dining Room, the King and Queen sat hand in hand. She knew he was unaware of the tightness of his grip. The Queen thought that if he squeezed any tighter, her hand would break. At the precise moment, the King turned to Magnor and nodded. Without hesitation, Magnor left the room heading for his chariot and the army that was standing in formation directly behind it. At the same moment, Magnor cracked the reins and the army began to move as one, the door to the Dining Room opened and Waldemar, Odella, and Quaine entered.

Patho took full advantage of having Jael locked in a cell in his workroom. Every possible insult that came to mind was quickly fired in Jael's direction. It only slightly bothered Patho that Jael hadn't reacted in any way since his arrival in the Pit. Patho was trying to come up with the best wording for an insult that compared the King with a platypus and a Temple Leader with no arms when the rumbling began. It was barely noticeable at first, but was quickly becoming loud enough to rattle the things laid out across his desk. Patho heard a commotion from people outside. "What in the Pit is going on out here?!" he yelled, as he swung open the door. Either no one was sure or they were all too panicked to answer him.

He slammed the door shut as the rumbling grew louder and louder. And then, from out of nowhere, there was suddenly a radiating light that began to fill the room. It seemed to be getting brighter with each second. In fact, it was getting very bright, very quickly. Patho spun around and realized that the light was coming from Jael's cell. With an echoing crash, the cell door flew off its hinges. It slammed into the door to the workroom and sent both doors flying.

"NO!!" shrieked Patho. "You can't leave! You're stuck here forever! You are mine! You failed to honor your request for forgiveness; that means YOU ARE MINE!"

Jael stepped out of the cell and looked Patho directly in the eyes. "I am not yours. I never made a request for forgiveness. I had no reason to ever ask for it."

"But you left the Kingdom, you turned your back on the King!" Patho screeched over the sound of the rumbling, which was now so close that the entire Pit was vibrating. "You, Quaine, and Palti, you are all MINE!"

"You are right, I did leave the Kingdom. But I did not leave it for myself, and I NEVER turned my back on my Father! I left so that you could no longer succeed in preventing any of the Fallen Souls from finding their way home!" Jael continued to make his way towards the exit.

Patho jumped in front of Jael in an effort to stop him. "But the sacrifices," Patho argued in desperation, "they mean nothing to the Humans anymore!"

"You may have greatly corrupted the sacrifices that the Fallen Souls were making to the King, but the King has now made a sacrifice in their place. It is for anyone and everyone who is willing to accept it." Jael stood directly in front of Patho. From outside, Jael heard Magnor call his name. Patho heard it as well.

"But you can't leave! You are no different than anyone else. You are subject to the Laws just like every other Fallen Soul!" Patho cried.

"I am here because I was subject to those Laws. I'm leaving because I have fulfilled them." With that Jael walked out of the Pit. Patho stood in disbelief of what was unfolding before him. He watched as Jael entered the King's chariot. He began to jerk uncontrollably. Patho watched as Magnor made his way to the front of the army, and with shouts of triumph he led the charge back to the Kingdom. As the sight of them grew smaller in the distance, Abaddon and Serpent appeared in the shattered doorway.

"We have..." Abaddon's sentence was interrupted by a well-aimed brick exploding against the wall just above his head. Abaddon looked at Serpent in hopes that Serpent would deliver the news. Serpent stood expressionless; he had no intention of assisting. Looking back at Patho he said, "We have information you need to hear."

Serpent hissed a laugh. "You have another problem on your hands."

Patho glanced up, looking extremely disheveled and with an evil hatred in his eyes. Abaddon forced out the words, "Apparently, Quaine has already returned to the Kingdom."

"What!? How?!" Patho screeched.

"Timar, the Human we thought was doing our bidding with the Temple Leaders – it appears that he was Quaine." Serpent said without a hint of surprise or disappointment. Patho glared at him with a blazing hatred. Serpent froze. He stared back. He watched in disturbed fascination as Patho's appearance began to change right in front of him. Within seconds Patho had become something very similar to - Serpent. Serpent couldn't take his eyes off Patho. His curiosity and fascination piqued as Patho continued to transform until he was something even more other - than the Others. Patho began to shake and twitch. Abaddon was desperately evaluating possible escape routes. Serpent grinned.

"Make sure that Palti is guarded at all times." Patho seethed as he made his way over to Abaddon. Standing inches away he shouted, "I will not lose another one! You do know where Palti is?"

Abaddon stood motionless, Patho's warm repulsive breath circling around him. Abaddon didn't bother hoping that Serpent would save him from what he was about to say. "They've lost track of Palti." Abaddon sprinted through the doorway and didn't stop until he reached the furthest edges of the Pit. Patho's scream had started the moment the words had left his lips. He stood gasping for air, looking out into the Darkness as the horrible sound of Patho's anger continued to bounce around the walls of the Pit.

The Kingdom waited in all of its splendor
for the return of their Prince.

The scream finally stopped. Patho stood in his broken office, seething with rage. The fact that Serpent hadn't reacted at all only infuriated him more.

"So," Serpent said without blinking. "Now what, O' Brilliant Angel of Light?"

Cast of Characters

The Seven Brothers

Palti: Prince, eldest son who is missing since the great departure

Magnor: Prince, Commander over the King's Army

Carasi: Prince, overseer of the daily operations of the Kingdom

Ferrul: Prince, shares the responsibility of overseer of the of the Kingdom with Carasi

Quaine: Prince, left the Kingdom with Patho

Konnory: Prince, philosopher and first male human in Turayn

Jael: Prince, youngest of the seven brothers

The King & Queen: rulers over the Kingdom

Patho: the great deceiver

Others: Kingdom dwellers that left the Kingdom prior to Patho's departure

Watchers & Messangers: Angels

Stories retold in this book:

Creation: Genesis 1 & 2

Cain & Abel: Genesis 4

Gilli: Enoch - Genesis 5:24

Latzof: Noah - Genesis 5, 6 & 7

Nadav: Joseph - Genesis 37 - 50

Hadad: David - 1 & 2 Samuel

Lior: Elijah - 1 King 18

Ram: Daniel - Daniel 6

Ada: Esther - Book of Esther

Baptizer: John the Baptist - Matthew 3

The stories told while Jael was in Turayn can be found in the four gospels.

www.ingramcontent.com/pod-product-compliance
Lightning Source LLC
Chambersburg PA
CBHW051330250626
47155CB00007B/2528